Scribe Publications
I SAY TOMATO

Katie Wall is an Australian actress. She has appeared in films and TV series, including *Clubland*, *My Year without Sex*, *Underbelly 2*, *Dirt Game*, *Noise* and *Love My Way*. She won an AFI Award for Best Supporting Actress for *Marking Time*. *I Say Tomato* is her first novel.

I SAY TOMATO

Katie Wall

SCRIBE
Melbourne

Scribe Publications Pty Ltd
PO Box 523
Carlton North, Victoria, Australia 3054
Email: info@scribepub.com.au

First published by Scribe 2010

Cover design by Neryl Walker
Typeset in 11.75/15 pt Adobe Caslon Pro by the publisher
Printed and bound in Australia by Griffin Press. Only wood grown
from sustainable regrowth forests is used in the manufacture of
paper found in this book.

National Library of Australia
Cataloguing-in-Publication data

Wall, Katie

I Say Tomato

9781921640407 (pbk.)

A823.4

www.scribepublications.com.au

For Conor

I smile every time the tag on the car windscreen beeps when I'm going through toll areas.

If I visit a public toilet block more than once I always stay loyal to the same cubicle.

The length of my bath can measure my level of happiness on any given day. The shorter, the happier.

Every time I wait in a line, I count in a loop from twenty backwards in my head.

Some mornings I take two of my once-a-day multivitamins, and sometimes I skip them altogether.

I love the space of time that is created when plans are cancelled at the last minute.

Sometimes I walk when the sign says *Don't Walk*.

These are my answers on standby to questions I am waiting to be asked. This is what is running through my head as I am lying under a tree in shavasana at the end of my free yoga class in the park. I have been overseas alone for a week now and am very ready for a conversation that goes deeper than asking for directions.

'Be at one with the sun, the wind and this beautiful park,' the yoga teacher says as she walks around covering over groundhogs' burrows with her foot. Her white thongs are slowly getting more and more red mud on them, which I hope will wash off. She has fake breasts and a slightly stunned, excited look on her face — permanently.

In unison we breathe in love and reach for the sky. Then we let it all go, breathe out and repeat after our teacher a loud 'fuck you' to negativity. We breathe in again and say 'fuck you' to the baggage that we no longer need. The last 'fuck you' is to all of those murky mind patterns that no longer define us. The class finishes with rapturous applause, hugs and cheering. A man near me in bike pants gives me an eager smile that I pretend not to notice so as not to get myself involved in an impromptu hug.

Hello, enthusiasm. Hello, Hollywood. The best-looking male and female from every high school and drama school on the planet have been plucked from their hometowns and dropped here in LA, with a new, younger truckload arriving every day.

Back at my rented 'fully furnished boutique studio apartment in the heart of Hollywood' I stare out the window, which faces a brick wall. I wonder what my view would have been if I'd ended up in India instead of here. I had to make a quick exit out of Sydney, and while looking up flights to Mumbai, I spoke to my Australian agent who suggested I choose LA instead. Seeing as the flight was half the price of the one to India, here I am.

I make a cup of tea and take it and my laptop up two floors, then down a long hallway to steal the internet from apartment number 521, which is next door to the laundry. The laundry smells like washing powder, families and home, which couldn't be further from this sterile, pigeon-coop-type living.

I sit on one of the dryers, which is still warm, and look at the brief for my first American screen test for the coming afternoon. I am going for the part of the 'jogger' in a Nike commercial. Description of jogger: curvy but fit body, and a beautiful smile. How on earth did I end up being put up for parts as an extra? I make it to the bottom of the page and realise why: the fee is enough to buy a studio apartment in Potts Point. I flick over to Facebook and read: *Facebook helps you connect and share with the people in your life.* I completely disagree. I find it the loneliest concept I have ever come across. It's as if I'm looking through thick glass into a party I'm not invited to.

I spot an unread message in my inbox from George Shores. He's a Sydney actor who played my love interest on a television series a few years ago.

Hey I hear you are in town — you up for a drink? 3234239388 x

The dress code for every audition here is simply to look as hot as possible; a good amount of cleavage supposedly boosts your chances for a call back. I whip on a ridiculously padded bra, cringe at my reflection in the mirror and jump in the car.

I walk into a holding pen crammed with women with eminent facial structure. It is silent, and a swarm of last-minute nerves have just flown in and landed all over me. Damn. I take a seat and try to breathe slowly. I avoid eye contact because my nerves are loud ones, the kind that blare out of your eyes. At least I don't have any lines! I don't have to do the accent, which for me is like walking on my hands at the best of times.

The room continues to fill up and every time a new girl walks in she signs the book at the door. Shit, should I have signed it? Should I ask someone? I don't want everyone to think I don't know what I'm doing. Should I ask in an American accent? What if it comes out wrong? I make my way up to the book and see a column for names, agents and arrival times.

'Excuse me?' I say to one of the girls. (It comes out even more Australian than my normal accent.) 'Does everyone have to sign this book?'

'Yeah, and write down the time you arrived. Everyone here has the same call-time to audition, but it goes in order of who arrives first.' I have never come across that in Australia.

I am in trainers; everyone else is in some form of high heel. Finally, after almost an hour my name comes up. I walk into the room and am briefly introduced to the casting assistant and camera operator. No matter what the audition is for, or what the job is, whenever 'action' is called I am instantly faced with what I really think of myself in that moment. I don't know what it is about that one word, but it can get you to a point that usually takes twenty therapy sessions. I am shitting myself. I jog on the spot, trying to look as calm as possible, but feel like I'm driving with the handbrake on. I am complimented on my name, thanked and am out within about one minute flat.

I jump back into my hired silver PT Cruiser and drive home. At the traffic lights, I get my phone out to call George to arrange our drink. My heart speeds up double time. I hang up just before it starts ringing. What is wrong with me? I don't even fancy him. It's a casual drink with an old friend, for goodness sake. An old friend that I have pashed. It was on a TV show — it doesn't count. I call again. It's ringing. My breath is short. Please don't let a shaky voice come out.

'Hello?'

'George, it's Sunny.' We're okay, not too shaky Stevens.

'Oh, darlin', so good to hear your voice. What's happening?'

'I just went to an audition for a "jogging woman", but I don't think my boobs are big enough. It said in the character breakdown "curvy body".'

'Spewin'.'

'Yeah, I am. So things are going really well for me so far. What about you?'

'Yeah, I'm good. Looks like some private funding is about to come through for my short film, and I've landed a sick pad in Echo Park. It belongs to a director who is out of town for a few months.'

'Oh shit, just a sec, there's a cop.' I drop my phone in my lap till he passes.

'You know it's legal to talk on your phone while driving here?' George says as I put the phone back up to my ear.

'Bullshit.'

'It is. The phone companies would lose too much money if it were illegal. Anyway, you should come and check out my new place. What are you doing tonight? How about a jacuzzi?'

'Um, sure, yeah, why not, I'm free. What time should I come?'

'I'll be back around 7.30, so anytime after that. I'll get some takeaway and we can watch cable on demand.'

'Okay. How do I get there? You have to give me directions to avoid freeways, because I can't drive on them.'

'Why not?'

'Because they're terrifying.'

And the deal is done. Simple as that. Yikes.

'Wow-wee. I bet this place helps pull chicks,' I say.

'It certainly does,' George says, and pretends to root a girl from behind up against the kitchen bench.

It's a big place, but has a cosy ski-lodge feel to it. It's full of ornamental treasures, which I assume are from film sets, from string puppets to a Native American headdress.

We make our way through spring rolls, lemon chicken, beef in black-bean sauce, fried rice, an episode of *Curb Your Enthusiasm*, and almost two bottles of wine. We get onto the subject of the television show we were on, and George says he still blames me for nearly getting him fired. We both have quite a serious problem with laughing when we're not allowed to, and the two of us in a scene together was always dangerous.

We go and hop into the jacuzzi on the deck looking out onto the hills. George can't get the bubbles working, which is kind of awkward. We are basically sitting in a hot bath together in our cossies. He uses the lack of bubbles as an excuse to move on to bubbly.

'I heard you and Tobey broke up. I'm sorry to hear that. How was it, the whole break-up thing?' George asks.

'You know, pretty fucked. It was like our relationship

all of a sudden got cancer, the quick kind.'

'I have to say, you had men all over Sydney lighting candles the day you went back on the market.'

'What do you mean by that?'

'It was a momentous time in history. There was suddenly hope for all the men out there that they may get to bed you after all. You weren't lost to the dark side of boring, old, shacked-up people. A lot of men I knew marked it with a moment of silence and lit a candle in celebration of this hope.'

'You're so full of shit.'

'I am not; I lit two.'

'Get out.'

'It's true! I've always had the horn for you.'

'The horn? What does that mean?'

'Never you mind.'

We share a cigarette and he talks me through the story of his short film, which sounds really good, and I go on to tell him about my new American manager. Mid-sentence I feel a foot touch mine underwater. No, it is not a brush-past mistake.

'Don't you dare try and crack on.'

'What?' he asks, keeping his foot there.

'Don't give me "What?" I feel the old lingering foot.'

'Innocent, innocent. Carry on. You were saying?'

I smile. 'Well,' I say, 'I couldn't believe it when I first went to meet my manager. Her office looks like the bloody White House.'

Foot still there. I move mine away. His follows and finds mine again. I jump out and he leaps out after me. He grabs me and steps back on my right foot. I don't realise how drunk I am until I am standing. We stop for a moment. The air is thick with teenage silence. He makes me slow dance to 'Shelter' by Ray LaMontagne, which is blaring through the impeccable sound system.

'Are we going to have sex tonight?' he asks.

'No, George, we definitely are not.'

'But we dance this well together. That translates in the sack, you know.'

'Answer's still no.'

'Give me one good reason why not.'

'You've slept with nearly every actress in Sydney.'

'All the more reason! Wouldn't want to be left out, would you? Give me a better reason.'

'You call actresses "mattresses".'

'If you were a mattress you would be a thick, luxurious, latex pocket-spring one.'

'You are trying to get me into bed by saying if I was a mattress I would be a thick one?'

'Yep. Real natural sweet-talker, aren't I?'

'You are, but the answer is still no.' We continue to dance and I can smell Old Spice on his neck. He is not conventionally handsome but has a knowing twinkle in his eyes, with just a hint of damage, which keeps both directors and beautiful women knocking on his door.

'I have not slept with every actress in Sydney,' he says.

'Don't you dare try and deny the fact you are a get around round round.'

'I just haven't found the right one yet. They've all turned out to be psychos.'

The slow song ends and I break away to go to the bathroom. I stumble on my way. I sit on the toilet with my head in my hands. The room is spinning. Damn. I am way too drunk to drive, and I am a very expensive cab fare away from home. I wash my face and gulp from the tap. I go into the kitchen and get a big glass of water.

'Hey, I'm sorry for being sleazy. Couldn't help myself — I'm a shocker. Here punch my arm.' I do. Really hard. 'Shit, that was like a man's punch! That will bruise. Let's go out dancing. I know a great dingy little dive bar just down the road from here.'

'Nup. I feel sick.'

'What, from the drinks? You've had like three.'

'I've had about six or seven. I usually spew by my fourth.'

'Oh, you poor thing, here.' He sits me down and grabs my foot and presses a pressure point that is supposed to sober you up.

'It's not working; it's making me even more nauseous.'

'Oh, shut up. It's meant to take five minutes.'

'Five minutes! That's ages.'

'Be patient. Here I'll put on my new show-reel for you to watch while you wait. By the end of it you will definitely sober up.'

The music and scenes he has chosen are really good. There is a raunchy one of the two of us pashing in a car. I get an about-to-spew wave. I snatch my foot away and stand up and go to the toilet. It's like a waterfall. A never-ending waterfall of lemon chicken. I am such an idiot. Why did I drink that much?

When it is finally all over I clean up the mess I have made and look at myself in the mirror. What am I doing here? What am I doing with a different man? I want to go home. My eyes are bloodshot, I have a few bits of spew in the front of my hair, wet splashes on my top, and mascara streaked down my face and onto my neck. I am the most revolting person.

'Did you just chuck?' he yells through the door.

'Maybe,' I say in the tiniest voice.

'You decent?' he asks, opening the door. 'Wow, look at you.'

'Can you get out, please?'

'Do you want to borrow some clothes?'

'Um, yes. That would be good.'

I scrub my face till it's red raw, then remember I didn't bring my make-up bag. Oh crap. He comes back with clothes and a toothbrush still in its packet.

'Do you have a stash of these for all your dirty stopouts?' I ask, and he doesn't answer.

I have a shower, then creep out and sit on the lounge.

'Sorry, I'm embarrassed,' I say.

'Don't be. Are you feeling any better?'

'Yeah, heaps better actually.'

'Better enough to go out to a bar?'

'George, no, I can't go. If you want to go, go ahead.'

'Come on, you will love it, I promise. When we get there I'll get you a shot of this herbal liqueur that will make you feel a million dollars.'

'Really, I couldn't be further from coming.'

'Please. Is there anything in the world I could do to get you to come?'

'Wear that.' I point to a bear head on a hat rack that is the top part of a bear costume.

'Okay.' He grabs it and puts it on. 'Let's go.'

'You're not really going to wear it into the bar.'

'You want to bet?'

'Okay, you have to wear it the entire time we are out of the house. Under no circumstance can you take it off.

If you do I will leave. Okay?'

Uh-oh, this means I have to leave the house with no make-up, in George's clothes.

We walk out the front door and George grabs a little girl's pushbike with flowers on the front basket and spokey dokies on the wheels.

'Jump on,' he says.

'No way, José. Why don't we just walk?'

'Way too far. You can't walk to anything in LA.'

'Then we'll get a cab.'

'No cabs in LA.'

I climb onto the handlebars. We take off, turn a corner and go down a massive hill, which makes my bottom slip forward into the basket. I scream and swear all the way down.

I feel like I am freefalling.

I have a man behind me that isn't Tobey and I don't like it at all.

'Ah! I lost a thong!' I yell.

'Oh well!'

'No, stop. George, go back, please!' I love my electric-blue Havaianas.

'Too late! I can't pedal back up the hill now; we'll get it on the way back.'

'Can you even see through that bear head?'

'Kind of.'

We dump the bike around the corner from the bar, and I roll down the tracksuit pants I am wearing, to cover my one bare foot. We arrive and the bouncer says George is not allowed in with his bear head on. He goes to take it off.

'Don't you dare,' I say to him, then ask the bouncer

why he won't let him in.

'Policy.'

'There can't be a policy against bear heads,' I say.

'Sorry, ma'am.'

We continue on back and forth. Bear head stands silently, a couple of feet away.

'Look, okay, I'll tell you the truth,' I say to the bouncer. 'My friend here got a nose job yesterday and has two black eyes and bruising all over his face. The only way we could come out tonight is if he wore this bear head.'

'Okay. In you go.'

We go downstairs and it is insanely cool. The room is full of sleeve tattoos, piercings and leather. It is dark and smoky and one wall is covered in graffiti. There is a huge old-world golden frame, with a DJ playing his records behind glass in an alcove in the wall. The interior is seemingly a shambles, but on closer inspection I see that it is very specifically choreographed chaos. There are a few people dancing and no one even really looks twice at bear head.

George tries to order drinks but can't be heard. He has to yell right into my ear, and I have to relay this to the unamused barman. We have shots of Fernet-Branca. George has his through a straw that we poke through one of the holes near his mouth. He is right: the herbal liqueur does make me feel a bit better.

I take my one thong off and we go and dance. For some reason George starts off with the 'Walk Like an Egyptian' dance, even though it doesn't go with the music. I shake my head at him, but he continues on with it for quite a while, pausing only to take a sip of his longneck beer that he also has to drink from a straw, which keeps falling back down into the bottle because they only had short straws at the bar.

Later, we find the bike is exactly where we left it.

'Can I take the bear off now?' George is drenched with sweat.

'Yes, you may.'

The journey home is a long one. There is lots of uphill, and pushing of the bike. George lends me one of his trainers, which is like a clown shoe on me. We don't find the missing thong.

'Do you want to stay tonight? I promise I won't crack on,' he says.

'Yeah, okay.'

We both jump into the king-size bed in the master bedroom. We have the French doors open and the breeze is heaven.

I stretch my arm up and see that it makes a shadow on the wall in front of me. In my old flat you could also do this. Every night Tobey and I used to put our hands up in the shape of ducks' faces and our shadows would kiss each other good night.

I make a duck's face with my hand and open and close its mouth. George then puts his hand up and makes some sort of crocodile shadow, which starts humping my duck. I immediately pull my hand down. George laughs, I don't.

'I don't sleep with that many girls, you know,' George says.

'Yes, you do. Do you ever fall for anyone?'

'I haven't for a long time, no.'

'Why do you think that is?'

'I had my heart broken once, and I don't think it can ever be fixed.' It is so rare to hear George speaking honestly. 'You know how if killer whales get taken into captivity, their dorsal fin flops over to one side?'

'I didn't know that, no.'

'And even if they are released back into the wild, their fin always stays flopped. I feel like I have a floppy fin,' he says quietly into the darkness.

'Are you talking about Jess?' I ask.

'Yep.'

'You will get over her, George. We're very resilient creatures.'

'I don't think I will, you know. I think about her almost every day.'

'How long has it been now, since you broke up?'

'Almost two years.'

'Shit that's a while.'

'Sure is. Night, spewie,' he says.

'Night.'

The next morning I wake up after a terrible sleep. Without Tobey's snoring, sleep has been difficult, like trying to dance to silence.

I find my way back to my studio, and while walking along the hallway I look into a few apartments that have their doors open. Mostly I see single, yucky-looking men watching television. God, this is like living in a male prison.

I try calling Nina, one of my best friends from Australia, who has been living in LA for the last three years. She has been out of town for the last week, on a camping trip with her 'not-boyfriend', Two-day Ray, and is arriving back today. Her phone goes through to her message bank, so I try twice more, then leave a message.

I hop into a bath that is too hot and makes my skin dark red. I listen to Joni Mitchell on my iPod, and peel an orange with fingers that are crinkly. I stay in until the water is almost cold.

Finally, I yank myself out and go on a grocery-shopping trip. I walk into Whole Foods, a health-food paradise that is bigger than most large Australian supermarkets. I start growing slightly suspicious after sampling bread that claims to be fat, sugar and wheat free, yet tastes like sponge cake. I have a moment of deliberation, but decide it's easier to believe the claims, and continue to fill my basket.

On the way back to my car I see what looks like a person hunched over in the gutter making a moaning noise. My first thought is that he must be homeless, but on closer inspection I see white linen pants, expensive glasses and paper shopping bags from Whole Foods on the ground next to him.

'Excuse me, are you alright?' I ask.

'Oh dear, my silly old back has slipped out,' the man says, sitting in a contorted position. He would have to be in his late sixties or early seventies. He has kind eyes and smells of sandalwood.

'Well, the same sort of thing happens to me. You're okay, you're going to be fine.' I kneel down on the ground with him. 'Just breathe.'

'Oh dear, I am so sorry about this. I am so sorry to bother you. This has never happened to me in public before. It usually locks when I'm in bed, or at home, but maybe the groceries were a little too heavy for me.'

'Don't apologise. I am so happy to help you. My name is Sunny. What's yours?'

'Albert Sinkway. Pleased to meet you. This is so kind of you to help me.'

'Now let's see if we can sit you up.' I very slowly move him to a seated position. He has watery eyes, and is quivering slightly. I know this specific pain so well myself. 'Keep breathing deeply. When you stop, that's when your body freezes. Now where do you live?'

'In the Hollywood Hills. I am parked just there.'

He points.

'We're going to get you into my car, lying down along the back seat, and I'm going to take you home.'

'Oh dear, no, love. I don't want to trouble you further. If you could just call me a taxi or maybe an ambulance they can take me from here.'

'No, don't be ridiculous.'

I drive right up alongside him and it takes us a good ten minutes to get him into my car, all in slow motion. He repeats the word 'sorry' and I repeat the word 'breathe' over and over, as if I am coaching a woman through labour.

We make our way to his place, and it is the classic Hollywood Hills home. I get him inside and lay him down on the lounge. Covered in sweat, he looks like a baby bird that has been stuck in a thunderstorm.

'Now is there anyone I can call for you? Family?' I ask him.

'Well, it's only me here actually; my wife passed nine months ago.'

'I am so sorry to hear that.'

'Thank you, dear.'

I call his chiropractor, who says he will be over shortly. I insist on staying with Albert until he arrives, and go to the kitchen to make him a cup of tea.

'I have never seen a tea collection like this,' I say as I open a whole cupboard dedicated to tea.

'Oh that's all Pearl, my wife. She would find any excuse for a cuppa. Good news, bad news, a reward after doing a chore, and insisted everyone around her keep up with her intake. She lived for tea parties. Very social woman, Pearl.'

I look at him, and can see how much he loved her.

'I love tea, too,' I say.

'English, are you?'

We chat about me, and what I am doing here. I tell him I've gone from living on the beach in Sydney, to being dropped smack bang in the middle of ghetto Hollywood, like a cat that has been thrown into a swimming pool.

The chiropractor arrives, examines Albert and says he has a muscle spasm, which should improve with some adjustments, painkillers and a good night's sleep.

I try Nina again, who finally answers. We plan to meet, just near Albert's car, so I can drop it home for him.

I arrive at Milk, a café on Beverly Boulevard. She is already there and jumps up and runs into a tight hug, which she pulls out of and rearranges.

'You have to hug with your left arm on top so our hearts touch,' she says.

It's been a while since I've been hugged. We lived together for years in Sydney, and have the kind of friendship where you can pick off each other's plates without asking. In the ten years I have known her, she has always worn Coco Chanel Mademoiselle perfume, and too many jingling bracelets up both arms. She has a pretty face, long curly hair, and reminds me of Kate Hudson's character from the film *Almost Famous*. We talk over each other and try to fit three years' worth of absence into the present moment. We order Strawberry Shortcake milkshakes that are made up of vanilla ice cream, strawberries, malted milk, strawberry sorbet and buttery crunchy cookie crumbles.

'I've used up my dessert credits for the next month on this one milkshake, but my god was it worth it,' Nina says. She has adopted some American speech patterns and a slight accent.

Nina is also an actress, and the most obsessive person I have ever met. She admits she lies to her therapist, and has been on a diet for as long as I've known her. She is very open about food and men being her two drugs of choice.

She goes on to tell me about her disastrous camping trip, where she fought with Two-day Ray the entire time. He is a drummer from a very well-known rock band, and got his name because he told her he loved her after they had only known each other for two days. They met at a petrol station when they were both filling up their cars. They made eye contact, and Two-day Ray started doing a sexual-type motion with the petrol pump. I think I would have called the police, but Nina got his number.

I have only seen him in photos: he is heavily tattooed; has dyed-black, shoulder-length hair (vomit); and his body looks as though it has seen five lifetimes in its one. He is married but is still promising he will break it off with his wife and belong exclusively to Nina. She's been waiting for over a year.

'Shit, Sunny! This guy must be loaded. Is he hot?' Nina says when she sees Albert's car.

'He's pushing seventy, but yeah, I think he would have been handsome in his heyday.'

'What? You're making me schlep all over LA for some guy without either of us potentially getting laid?

Are you serious?'

She drives my car and I drive Albert's back to his place. I then drop her back to her car and sit and watch her as she drives off.

She has changed in ways that are impossible to detect through phone or email. It's something in her eyes; she has a resigned edge to her that was never there before. She worked on two long-running television shows in Australia, but since being here she hasn't had one acting job.

So many Australian actors I know have got themselves into major debt in order to be here, and will struggle for the rest of their lives to pay that money back. Hollywood is like one big casino, and actors the compulsive gamblers. Maybe they've stayed here too long and lost too much money, which makes them feel like they can't leave till they hit the jackpot. Maybe they're all holding out for the one time they press the button and all the dollar signs line up and the music plays.

I head back to Albert's place. He's still in with the chiropractor, so I take a little wander through the house. It's 1920s, white, light and fresh. There are grand flower arrangements in most rooms, and his book collection is extraordinary. I head out towards the pool area; there is a waterfall, a line of sun beds, and a view of the hills. I have a sticky beak into the windows of the outhouse. You really can live beautifully here with enough money. On my way back inside, I stop at a line of framed movie posters. They are tacky-looking, from the '70s and '80s with Albert's name credited under 'Writer'.

I go upstairs to Albert's room just as the chiropractor is finishing and packing up his table. I knock on the open bedroom door.

'Come in.' Albert smiles. He lies on his bed, still with a slightly pained look on his face.

'So you're a screenwriter, is that what you do?' I ask as I sit down on a chair next to his bed.

'Once upon a time I sold some dog-awful scripts, yes. No one wanted to touch the good ones, so I sold out and gave them what they wanted.'

'That's amazing! I'm sure they weren't awful. So are you famous?'

'No, I'm not. Are you?'

'No.'

Albert pays the chiropractor, and I excuse myself and go to the bathroom.

While washing my hands in Albert's ensuite I see something that stops my breath. There are two toothbrushes in the holder. One pink, and one blue. Was the pink one Pearl's, which he hasn't been able to throw in the bin? I sit back down on the toilet and feel a wave coming up from my toes to my chest. I catch it in my breath. I try to hold back the tears that are pressing up against the floodgate but I can't. A little sob escapes. My face trembles; I bite my lip, and dig my nails into my palms to try to regain some sort of control, but it doesn't really help. Oh shit, my mascara has run. He is going to think I am some kind of depressive psycho.

'Oh, Albert, I am so sorry, I just had a bit of a cry in your bathroom. You don't even know me — you probably think I'm mad.'

'Is everything okay?'

'Yeah, yeah, I'm fine. Sorry.'

'Oh don't apologise, dear girl. These walls are no strangers to tears. This last year I have cried more than I thought possible.'

'I am so sorry about Pearl. I have never really experienced death, so I can't even begin to imagine what you are going through. What was it like, her dying?' He looks at me for a long moment. 'I can't believe I just asked that. That was totally out of line.'

'No, no, I like that you asked me. You are the first person to actually ask that question. Most people put death in the too-hard basket, and send over-the-top bunches of flowers to overcompensate for the fact they don't want to be anywhere near it. I expected the people close to me to step up and hold my hand all the way through, but they didn't. I don't blame them; I've done the same thing myself. People in this country don't want to be anywhere near death. No one will even say that word. You have to say "passed" so as not to offend anyone.'

'How did she die?'

'Lung cancer. Never touched a cigarette, not even one puff. When she was first diagnosed she thought there had to be some kind of mistake, but after that she was incredibly accepting. The doctors gave her six months and she was gone within seven. She exited this world with such grace, and prepared for her death like it was another one of her little projects. She was in bed for the final six weeks, but up until that time she was fighting fit. She even threw herself a goodbye party here at the house. It was a great evening.'

'Oh, wow. She sounds amazing, Albert. Life is big, isn't it?'

'It certainly is.'

We sit, smiling in silence. I then ask Albert if he needs anything and whether I can get him some dinner.

'The painkillers I need are in a jar in my bathroom cabinet. You can simply bring the whole jar in, if you don't mind, and my dinner is already made up: it just needs defrosting in the microwave for ten minutes. It's in the freezer on the top right in a blue tupperware container.'

As I watch the numbers count backwards on the microwave's screen, I wonder if Pearl made this meal. I take Albert what looks like pumpkin soup on a tray and ask if I can borrow a couple of books. He insists I take absolutely anything I want from the entire house. He says he would be left for dead on that street corner if it weren't for me.

Next morning I call Albert, who says he is feeling much better. I head to my first Bikram yoga class, otherwise known as the McDonald's of yoga. There are twenty-six postures done in forty-one-degree heat. As I open the door to the classroom I take a deep breath of thick air, which makes me feel like I am trying to breathe underwater. I join the other bodies and lie down on my mat, and am quickly informed by the girl to my right that I am lying in the wrong direction; apparently in India it's offensive to expose the bottom of your feet to the instructor.

When it is time to begin, our teacher, who is a camp, comedian type, makes a grand entrance. I get the feeling it would take a lot more than the bottoms of feet to offend him. He tests out his material on the class between postures, and I suspect he was drawn to teaching Bikram yoga because it gives him a guaranteed audience that can't leave the room for ninety minutes. Each posture is held for between ten seconds and a minute, and for each one we are told which area we are targeting in terms of ridding ourselves of fat. He says this series is a game of Simon Says in hell, and that it removes loose screws from the mind. Both of these things I agree with, and I emerge feeling like I have shed a layer and decide to buy a ten-class pass.

I join the queue at Pinkberry, an incredibly popular frozen-yoghurt café. You can choose from original or green-tea flavour, and there is a choice of toppings, from fruit to granola. It's one big fat lie: it's basically tangy ice cream, but somehow the words 'yoghurt' and 'fruit' put it into the health-food category. Again, easier to just believe the claims. I grab two containers of original yoghurt overflowing with toppings and head to Albert's.

He looks like a different man; there's a real elegance about him. We go and sit outside to eat our dessert, Albert on a sun bed and me with my legs dangling in the pool. The jasmine smells exquisite, and I don't feel like I am in America at all.

'Do you have any kids?' I ask.

'No, we weren't able to have children. We made up for it in our own ways though. Do you have brothers and sisters?'

'Three sisters.'

'Your lucky parents! Where do you sit?'

'I'm in the middle. The twins are the youngest, and I have an older sister. We're all really close in age.'

'What a handful!'

'Yeah, we were. Mum pretty much did it all on her own, too. Dad had an affair a few years after the twins were born, and none of us have had contact with him since.'

'Was that at your mother's request? Not to be in

contact with your father?'

'Um, no, I don't think so. All us girls banded together so tightly after they split up, and being in contact with him was never really an option.'

'Do you remember him?'

'Yeah, kind of. I remember leaving the city. After the affair Mum piled us in the car and drove us to a little country town called Bellingen, which is near the east coast of Australia. She bought a big old farmhouse, where she still lives now.'

'She sounds like a very strong woman.'

'Yeah, she's amazing. She's got her own business, too; it's an organic-bread company.'

'Good on her,' he says, smiling, then clears his throat. 'I have an idea. I would like to offer you my outhouse to stay in for as long as you require. It's private and comfortable. I think we need to get you out of the awful area you are in.'

'No, no, I couldn't. You could get a lot of money renting it out. I could never afford it.'

'Oh, don't be silly. I don't need the money. Besides, I could do with the company,' Albert says, and I get a rush of excitement all the way to my toes.

'I wouldn't feel right about not paying any rent.'

'Well, then that presents a problem. I will not accept money from you, Sunny.'

We finally agree on a deal: I'll cook the occasional meal in exchange for rent. I drive away smiling and let out a stupid-sounding squeal. I feel like I am in an American movie with a fairytale ending. Maybe it's true — maybe you can just be out grocery shopping in this city and stumble across a miracle.

Straight for seven steps, turn left for twelve steps, turn right for four steps, careful of the metal couch leg because it's easy to kick your toe on, turn left for four steps, then turn right for two steps. These are the directions to get to the toilet in the dark at our old flat. I wake up in my new outhouse in the middle of the night and slowly feel my way to the toilet. Do I replace this new mental map with the old one? Will I ever go back and live in the flat Tobey and I shared?

The following afternoon a test scene arrives in my inbox for a television pilot. The character I am to go for is a waitress described as highly intelligent, quirky, offbeat and, of course, incredibly beautiful. One shot of Maggie Gyllenhaal, one shot of Natalie Portman, with a twist of Scarlett Johansson is what they are looking for, apparently. The first scene is her singing karaoke; and the second one is set in a toilet cubicle: doing lines of cocaine with the male lead followed by a kiss.

My phone beeps; a text from George.

I have a huge bruise on my arm from where you punched me the other night. You are a man.

I smile and reply: *Well then that makes you gay because you tried to crack on.*

The lines sink in easily. I see my phone light up; another text from George wondering if I want to have dinner.

I can't tonight. I have lines to learn.

I'll come and help you.

I give him my address and he is on the doorstep within the hour.

While Albert and George chat, I go into the kitchen to start on the dinner preparations. I am glad no one is in the kitchen with me, because every time I cook I have my own imaginary cooking show going on in my head and I often mouth the directions as I go. I am doing an old faithful dish that is one of my signature gems: baked fish on a cabbage, carrot, coriander, mint and soba noodle salad with a lime, fish sauce, chilli, ginger and peanut dressing. I prepare the salad, marinate the fish, then take George up to my outhouse.

We start with the karaoke scene. I have chosen to sing 'Look Good in Leather', and begin very shakily. The character is meant to have a terrible voice, which is perfect for me.

The second scene we do in the toilet with the door closed to get a sense of the intimacy of the surroundings. It's separate from the bathroom and very squashy.

We pretend to snort cocaine in the confined space with scripts in hands and fumble our way through the scene. I know we are coming to the kiss and I have no idea what will happen. He moves closer to me, and as he scratches his beard I notice how many calluses he has on his hands. He has big weathered hands. I become aware of my breathing and can't seem to regulate it. His face moves closer to mine and there it is: the moment of choice.

The next thing I know, we are kissing. Our kissing is hungry and urgent and feels right in the same way eating a whole block of chocolate by yourself feels right. My memory of his taste is similar to the memory you have of taking your jumper off in the middle of the night. It is vague, planted somewhere in my subconscious, yet somehow familiar.

'Did I instigate that or did you?' I ask.

'Definitely you.'

'Oh my god, I'm sorry.' My face starts burning.

'You don't need to apologise.'

'Um, I should probably put the dinner on.'

Luckily my first meal for Albert is a hit. We drink a Californian pinot gris, which is surprisingly good. (I don't dare mention I found it on special for $2.99.)

'You sure have a natural talent for cooking,' Albert says.

'Anyone can cook; following a recipe is the same as following a road map,' I say.

'Did you follow a recipe to make this?' asks George, who doesn't make eye contact with me.

'No. I have a pretty good sense of direction when it comes to food,' I reply, not making eye contact with him either.

After dinner Albert suggests a poker game and insists we all have to wear hats. George is effortlessly charming with just the right level of self-deprecation. I start to wonder whether he has it in him to be a loyal husband and father, or whether he will always be a ladies' man.

'You alright?' George asks me.

'Yeah, just tired.'

The game finishes up, Albert wins by a mile, and then George leaves, giving me an awkward hug goodbye. Albert insists on the house rule: one person cooks, the other does the dishes. I dry.

'Do you think George is nice?' I ask.

'I do, yes. I think he thinks you are very nice, too.'

In bed that night, I watch the clock, and float between sleep and wake. I worry about my audition in the morning, and dream about Tobey.

Sitting in the waiting room I look at the posters of the films that this casting agent has obviously cast. They are big films, yet this is a very drab, dingy little office space. There seems to be a massive amount of money in the acting agencies themselves, yet almost no money in casting. There is no book to sign this time, and again I am made to wait for quite a while.

I go into the bathroom to put on a lucky last coat of mascara. Why is it that I have to open my mouth like a frowning blowfish every time I apply mascara? And it's not just me either: I see other women in bathrooms doing that face, too.

I am finally led into a small room. Great, I will be reading raunchy scenes opposite an overweight, red-haired woman in her fifties, who will also be operating the camera. I start with the song, which sounded a lot better in the shower this morning than it does now. Ouch, it is awful — I just can't quite manage to hit the right note. I decide to put us both out of our misery, and cut it a verse short.

Next up: the cocaine/pash scene. I work my way through and try to remember what I found in the scene the night before. In Australia you are almost always given notes and asked to try it again, but after my one take of each scene I am thanked and shown the door. Wham bam, thank you, ma'am. I wonder if it is an American thing, only to be given one take, or whether I was just plain terrible.

I drag myself along to a Bikram class to get me out of my head. I don't have my shorts and singlet with me, so I just wear my bra and underpants. They are sporty Bonds ones, but I still feel like I am offending everyone. Oh dear. It is way hotter than the last time, and my body clicks over into survival mode, which flushes away thoughts like: *Why did I kiss George last night? I'm a sleazy creep*, and *You just let another audition slip through to the keeper; it will only be a matter of time before your manager loses interest and dumps you.*

I finish the class and my mind feels as if it has zoomed out like a camera lens. As I am changing I check my phone: two missed calls from my manager. I have to meet the producers of the pilot tomorrow afternoon, at Fox Studios. Holy shitbags. Woo hoo! I am a valid human being after all. The world all of a sudden looks a different colour. A lighter colour. I text George.

I've been asked to meet the producers. Thank you so much for your help last night, and sorry I was sleazy x

I wait. No reply.

'Sunday Triggs.' I don't recognise the sound of my own voice. Those two single words make the boom gate at Fox Studios rise. I take a deep breath and try to follow the map to building C2. Oh crap — even with the air-conditioning on, there are sweat marks starting to develop under my arms. Maybe that guy I met who had injections in his armpits to stop the sweating wasn't such an idiot after all.

I am led into a room with seven other girls and two guys. No one is speaking and all eyes are fixed on lines on a page or closed. I decide to close mine and count backwards in my head until my name is called. I am led into a theatrette and introduced to the four producers and the director. The producers don't smile, and look like the cardboard cut-out moneymen that I imagined them to be. Luckily the director, named JC, has a bit more warmth about him.

The red-haired woman from the casting agency reads the toilet-cubicle scene opposite me. I know this scene backwards by now, but I've been told that I have to keep my script in hand whenever auditioning in America because, if not, they will think the performance is a finished product, and that's as good as you will get. I am thanked, and sent on my merry way.

That afternoon I get a call saying they would like me to 'test' in two days' time. Same scene, same place.

'But I've already tested, twice.'

'Not in front of thirty studio execs, you haven't,' my manager replies in her perfect all-American, singsong voice. 'Let's meet up at the Avalon at five.'

As I walk from my car to the Avalon Hotel in Beverly Hills I pass a dog draped in accessories, which makes my jaw instantly clench. It's the same kind of sudden infuriation I experience when someone puts a smiley face

KATIE WALL | 35

at the end of a text message or writes *LOL*. I really have tried to breathe through this irrational reaction, but it doesn't work. It seems that nearly everywhere I look in this city there is a dog in a diamanté collar or a candy-pink-striped tracksuit top with hood.

I arrive and spot my manager, Maryn, sitting by the window. She is very well groomed and could be described as attractive if photographed in the right light. She is on the phone but ends her call as soon as she sees me.

'We're all *so* excited about your call back! They love you!' she says, kissing me on the cheek. I think she has the highest-pitched voice I've ever heard.

'Oh, that's good.' I sit down opposite her.

'Look at your skirt! It's so cute! Where is it from?'

'Oh, nowhere. I just got it in an op-shop in Australia.'

'It's so great on you.'

We order drinks. I copy Maryn and get a boring old soda water with fresh lime.

'I have a lawyer that I'm going to put you in touch with so we can get you a visa,' she says. 'She's great. She'll have you sorted out in no time, then you can be here for the next few years without worrying. You're going to do so great out here, I know it.'

'Thanks,' I say with a smile that is sticky-taped on.

'We *have* to get some new headshots! I know a photographer who would be so good for you.'

'Oh, really? I only just got new ones done last year. Do you not like the one I have now?'

'It kinda seems like everyone from Australia has these black-and-white headshots, with really unhappy looks on their faces. We need something in colour, something really bright and sexy.'

'Okay.' I wonder whether she permanently talks at this pitch. Surely it's only when she's excited.

'So in terms of marketing you as a package, whose career do you see yourself having?'

'Um, I'm not really sure what you mean.'

'Okay, so in order to sell you, do you think I could say you are a Chloë Sevigny meets Kirsten Dunst?'

'Um, well, no, I don't see myself having their careers.'

'Why not?'

'Well, if I expected to have careers like theirs, I would end up sorely disappointed,' I say, laughing.

She looks confused. 'They're very successful, you know.'

'Yeah, I know. I just meant I could never be that famous.'

'Okay, girl, we have to get rid of that attitude! You can't afford not to back yourself. We have to keep your spirits up!'

She reaches across the table and takes hold of my hand. She looks at me sympathetically as if I've just said I've been contemplating suicide. 'Use this downtime to have fun! Go jogging in the canyon and make sure you do plenty of drop-in acting classes, in order to keep your tools sharp. I promise you it's only a matter of time before you book a job.'

I am relieved when we are finally interrupted by her next appointment, a pretty brunette who she also represents. Maryn throws some extra last-minute compliments at me as I leave, and manages to sustain her shrill pitch right till the end of meeting.

I call Nina and we go out for all-you-can-eat sushi for dinner. She is thrilled but admits she is equal parts jealous at the same time.

'You have gotten closer to a job in the one month you have been here, than I have in three years,' Nina says.

'It's just a test; it's no big deal, really.'

'Oh bullshit! It doesn't surprise me, Sunny. You have always been on the inner track of life.'

'What, and you've always been on the outer?'

'Yup.'

'Well, that's irrelevant, because the outside people get a head start.'

'I didn't.'

'How was your day?' I say, changing the subject.

'Interesting. My manager dumped me.'

'Oh god, I am so sorry.'

'It's fine, really. She was a bitch anyway. It was to be expected — she just lost interest in me. I was like a new dress to her: exciting to begin with, especially because I had them convinced I was mega-famous in Australia, but just as quickly I've been thrown onto the dirty washing pile and replaced with the next addition to the wardrobe.'

We drink sake, and the sushi that is being made in front of us by an old Japanese man with a long grey beard is melt-in-your-mouth amazing.

Nina tells me about the latest dramas at her current job behind the bar at a strip club called Thongs. (I did have to check with her and, no, the name has nothing to do with rubber footwear.) She isn't allowed to work legally in the US on her visa, so she works purely for cash tips with no wage. Apparently, because Nina is one of the untouchable women, the clients pay her more attention than they do the strippers, which a lot of the 'girls' aren't happy about. The clients regularly give her gifts, outrageous tips, and one guy even had to be banned from the bar because he became so desperately obsessed with her. On a good night she can take home up to six hundred dollars, which means she only has to work a few nights per week, leaving space during the day for auditions.

'So how are you really?' I ask.

'I'm actually really good. I do have a little help,' she says with a guilty smile. 'You can't tell anyone, but I have started taking antidepressants.'

'Oh my god.'

'I know it sounds like a big deal, but so many people in this country are on them. I was cleaning the house a little while ago with the TV on in the background and there was an ad for antidepressants, and I answered "yes" to every single question. I had not just three, but all ten symptoms on the checklist. At the end of the ad it said "you don't have to do it alone"— and I don't. I have done it alone for so long. I feel like for the first time in my life I am actually happy.'

'But it's manufactured happiness coming from a drug, not from yourself.'

'I disagree. I think the drug guides you in the darkness towards your own light. It takes you by the hand in the pitch-black, and places your hand in the hand of your own happiness; it acts like a little helper. I no longer have the "what have I done with my life?" tape playing over and over again in my head. It was like Chinese drip torture, Sunny; it has been for years. The tap is finally off and I'm finally out of prison.'

'Wow. Well, that's good news, I guess.'

'It's the same as botox: if you can't beat 'em join 'em.'

'You don't get botox, do you?'

'Yeah, along with almost every woman I know here.'

I can't believe it. Didn't we laugh at women who were stupid enough to get botox? Has it been that long since we've seen each other?

'Why do you have that look on your face?' Nina asks.

'I don't disagree with antidepressants. I think they definitely serve a purpose, but I don't know whether I agree with your "reuniting you with your own happiness" theory. I think they act as a bandaid and put everything in boxes under the bed to deal with at a later date. At some stage you will actually have to face that question: "What have you done with your life?" Whether you face it now or in ten years is up to you. I think the tablets you're taking are just buying you time.'

'Okay. Thank you for your very honest opinion.'

'Oh no, don't get upset.'

'I'm just so used to you backing me. I always thought if I robbed a bank you would sit me down for an extended tea-drinking session and make me feel like it was actually the right thing to do.'

'I heard someone say on the radio the other day that rationalisation is more important to the human condition than sex. In all honesty, don't you think that's kind of dangerous?'

'What?'

'The way people, women especially, justify each other's actions, even if they are actually wrong?'

'But wrong in whose opinion?'

'Well, for example, I think sleeping with a married

man is wrong.'

'Oh, well, thank you again for your very honest opinion. You have no idea about my relationship with Ray. I think you're only saying these things to be a bitch.'

'Why would I want to be a bitch? I'm saying them because I care about you. Nina, you've basically taken a "when in Rome" attitude to antidepressants.'

She stares at me, grabs her handbag, takes money out of her purse and throws it on the table.

'Please don't go; I'm sorry. Just sit down.' I grab her hand; she pulls away and leaves the restaurant.

I sit and finish off the sake on my own, pay the bill and leave.

On my way to the car I try calling Nina. It rings three times then goes to her message bank. I try a second, third and fourth time.

I get home, flop on the bed, and send her a 'sorry' text. I try to work out why I reacted so strongly to the antidepressants. Maybe I'm jealous she has her dripping tap turned off and wish mine could be, too.

I wake up and get ready for a drop-in acting class that comes 'highly recommended' by my manager. I search around in my drawer for socks and find a stray one of Tobey's, which I know would annoy him, as he is very obsessive when it comes to his socks. I put it on, and find a stray one of mine for the other foot.

I park my car across the road from the class in Studio City, and see a group of people milling outside the door, who are all obviously actors: they are just that bit too loud, and just that bit too animated.

We start by sitting around a table. Our teacher, Robin, who has a perm, asks us to go around the circle and introduce ourselves. The first guy's name is Eric, and tells us that he is a Gemini and enjoys long strolls along the beach at sunset, which has everyone in hysterics.

The next guy says, 'My name's Mark, and I'm an actor.'

The class responds by saying, 'Hi Mark,' as if we are in an AA meeting. Again, hysterical laughter.

The next girl, Georgia, raps her way through her introduction, then gets up out of her chair and does a breakdancing move. Lots of laughter and, this time, applause.

'Hi, I'm Sunny and I'm from Australia.' I get a few smiles, but it is awfully silent.

The introductions and laughter continue, while I pretend to be engrossed in searching through my bag. I find my lip balm and frantically apply it.

We are each given a piece of butcher's paper and a texta. We are asked to split the page into two columns: one column titled *Fears*; and the other, *Reality*. We are asked to write our fears in the first column, and the actual reality of the situation in the next column.

Robin explains that this exercise is done to dispel all of the unrealistic, negative thoughts we have that hold us back. I am not quite sure what to write, so I glance at the girl across from me's paper. She glimpses up just at the wrong time and looks at me as if she's caught me picking my nose.

We are asked to go around the table and read out one of our fears and the reality alongside it. A very large girl next to me named Amelia is asked to start. Her fear is that she won't be able to stick to her new Weight Watchers program and that she will be overweight forever. Then, under reality, she has written that she *will* stick to Weight Watchers and will have the body of Jamie Lee Curtis in *True Lies* within a year.

Everyone claps, and one guy yells out, 'Go girl!'

Next up, my turn.

'My fear is that I won't ever get another acting job, and the reality is I probably won't, seeing as ninety-nine per cent of actors are unemployed.'

'Okay, you have completely misunderstood the exercise,' Robin says with a passive-aggressive smile, flicking her frizzy hair out of her face.

'Oh. Which bit did I get wrong?'

'Under your reality column: it's still your fears talking, not an objective look at the reality of the situation.'

'So I got the reality bit wrong?'

'Why don't we ask the class? What do you think guys? Did Sunny get the reality bit wrong?'

Everyone says 'yes'.

'What is the reality then?' I ask.

'That, yes, you will get your dream acting job.'

'Okay. I'll change it.' I cross out my answer and write hers next to it.

The next guy starts on his fears, but Robin's scary eyes remain on me.

What? Why is she still looking at me? And why doesn't she use some kind of serum in her hair? It only costs about five dollars.

We are paired up and handed scenes to work on that we are to perform to the class. I am paired with Eric, and we go off into a corner to work on our scene, which is from *The Break-up*. It is a fight scene between Jennifer Aniston's and Vince Vaughn's characters. We do a read-through, and Eric yells really loudly from the first line all the way through to the end. We run it a couple more times: I try toning things down a bit, but Eric doesn't follow suit.

When it comes to our turn to read our scene for the class, it peaks in the first few seconds and we have nowhere to go. Eric gives the exact same autopilot performance, again yelling all the way through.

After watching our scene, Robin gushes when talking about Eric, saying he has a real presence, and that in observing this performance, he is the one that the eye is drawn to. She goes on to say that I have potential, yet she thinks I hold myself back. She also mentions she couldn't understand a lot of what I said.

As soon as the class finishes I am the first to get up and hand over the seventy-dollar fee. I use the bathroom on the way out, and in the mirror I see that I have quite a large piece of date from my breakfast bar stuck in between my two front teeth, which makes them look kind of rotten.

'Sunday Triggs.' The Fox Studios boom gate opens. I am taken to a room to look over a contract that Maryn has talked me through and has okayed me to sign. Apparently before a 'test' the actor is required to sign on to the television series, in case the pilot goes ahead.

I am about to hypothetically sign away the next seven years of my life, at thirty-five thousand dollars per week.

I am led into a small rehearsal space to workshop the scene with JC, the director, and again the red-haired casting agent will be reading with me. As I take a seat on a black leather armchair, red-hair lets me know the camera is already running. What does that mean? Should I try to be extra charismatic? Ah! I don't know how to be.

JC gives me some background on the character and we have a bit of a general chat. He has to ask me twice to speak up because he can't hear me. My god, I know I am coming across like a little field mouse but I can't seem to do anything about it.

'Think sex on every word,' he says, right before we start the scene.

I glance up at red-hair, who smiles. Again, I have my script in my hand, pretending not to know my lines; and again I am speaking in an accent, pretending to be American.

Next, I am led into the hallway outside the theatrette where there are three chairs set up. The other two chairs are filled with delicately pretty blondes, who are obviously my competition. They introduce themselves to me and sound as sweet as they look.

We sit in silence for what seems like a very long time. My wild-horse mind wriggles out of its bridle and starts going for a gallop, with thoughts like *You are a fraud, you shouldn't be here*, and *They must be desperate to fill the part, if they have got you in*. Then it starts bucking and pigrooting with *You are not pretty enough, and will never be in the league of girls like this*, and *No matter how much weight you lose you are too big-boned to ever be a leading lady*. I try counting backwards inside my head in the loudest voice I can.

Finally the executives stream past us. Some look at us and some don't. It's like we're sitting in a jail line-up, but in this case hoping to be picked. I'm first up.

I walk in and sit in the chair placed opposite my red-haired friend.

'And scene,' she says.

I try to conjure stored sexual images, but they don't come to me. Why can't they get a nice young man in to read? This is awful. I know I'm acting badly, yet there is nothing I can do about it.

Before I know it, the scene is over and I am told

to wait back out in the hallway. Both girls smile at me encouragingly but obviously they secretly hope I stuffed up. The next girl goes in and there is raucous laughter as soon as she walks into the room. Did she crack a joke? Or did she trip over? My evil mind hopes it was the latter.

After the third girl is finished, I am asked back in to read the scene again in an Australian accent. Woo hoo! This piece of direction is like Christmas to me. This time I read feeling free, as if I'm skinny dipping as opposed to swimming in a tracksuit.

7

I dream I'm driving on the wrong side of the road in the
dark with no headlights. I wake up in a panic and don't
want to be in this country anymore. It's still dark, but I
can't get back to sleep. I go down to the house and quietly
make myself a hot honey and lemon, then hop back into
bed and get on my computer. I check my email and there's
one from Tobey, sent via BlackBerry. We haven't been in
contact since our break-up, over a month ago. There is no
subject. I open it.

*Hey, have just locked myself out. Did you ever end up
hiding a spare key in the laundry? I couldn't find it.*

I do the maths: it's evening in Australia. I call him. It's
ringing. My heart gets faster and louder, and I suddenly
feel very cold.

'Hello?'

'Tobey, it's Sunny.'

'Hi. Um, can you hang on a second?'

'Yeah.'

'Can you order the steak for me?'

'You what?'

'Sorry, I'm out to dinner, I'm going outside ... Okay,
I'm out. I ended up breaking in.'

'How?' I ask.

'Through the bathroom window.'

'Don't tell me you scaled the ledge.'

'I scaled the ledge.'

'Oh my god, you could have killed yourself!'

'Anyway, how are you?'

'I'm okay.'

'What's been happening?' he asks in a formal tone that doesn't sound like him.

'Lots of auditions, I've been really busy, and it looks like there are a few promising things in the pipeline, which is good news.'

'Yeah, right. Do you like it there?'

'Yeah, I do. I love it. Actually I just told a lie; no, I don't really like it at all.' He laughs, his laugh sounds like home. It makes me want to curl up inside it. 'I miss Australia to be honest. I miss the beach.'

'I'm at the beach right now.'

'Are you? Which one?'

'North Bondi. I am having dinner at North Bondi Italian.'

'Oh, you're so lucky! Who with?'

'A friend.' Back to formal tone.

He's on a date. I get a sharp stab of jealousy. How could he be on a date? How can he be taking a girl that isn't me out to dinner? How can he be looking at a menu and deciding what to have with someone else? My throat tightens.

'Are you on a date?' I ask.

'It's not really a date, no.'

'Do you like her?' My voice sounds fierce.

'Sunny, I can't have this conversation with you right

now. I have to get off the phone.'

'Are you just going to hang up?'

'No.'

'So that's it. I'm out of sight out of mind, moving on to the next one.'

'You broke up with me.' His voice sounds detached.

'No, Tobey, you broke up with me.'

'For fuck's sake, here we go.'

'You asked me a big question and I didn't know the answer, so you broke up with me.'

'I've got to go.'

'Fine, bye.' I hang up on him before he can hang up on me.

I put my face into my pillow. What have I done? Have I lost him? Maybe I should just jump on a plane and go back and get him.

I ring Qantas to see if I can change my flight. There is a seat on a flight three days from now. What if I go back and there's a new girl in our flat? I have no idea what to do. I call one of my sisters and then my mum, who are both very sympathetic, but unfortunately neither of them make up my mind for me.

The sun is well and truly up. I grab a cigarette from my stash and hop into my car. Feeling numb, I drive along aimlessly, smoking and looking out the window onto the empty streets. No one ever walks anywhere in LA. What am I doing here? It's like being on a different planet, filled with orange-tinged people who smile all the time.

Hollywood: he promises you everything in the darkness, telling you true stories about going from *Home and Away* to the lead in a major American blockbuster in one effortless leap, yet I seem to awake to an empty bed. He slips away as if he had never existed. There is no number to call, and when you look him up there is no trace of him.

I get a call from my manager, who says it doesn't look like the pilot has gone our way. I proceed to have a week with no exercise, no auditions, no vegetables and no laughing. Tobey, George and Nina are not returning my calls. I check their Facebook pages and, yes, all three of them are still alive, happily commenting on other people's photos, updating their status, writing on other friends' walls and having a merry fucking time. Tobey's profile says *In a relationship*; he never changed it when we broke up. How convenient: now with this new slut on the scene he doesn't need to.

I find myself with lots of unstructured time alone spent staring, getting lost in shopping malls, smoking, eating pastry in any form, ordering items on the internet that promise to change my life, and receiving parking fines that leave me unfazed. I feel as if I'm stuck walking at a slow pace in a sea of people. All I want to do is climb up onto someone's shoulders and check how far the sea goes on — but I don't know anyone well enough to ask them and fear that I would be too heavy anyway.

I spill my whole container of powdered foundation on the bathroom floor, and don't bother to clean it up. I use it straight off the tiles, and wear it to bed. I am permanently bloated from the white flour in the pastry, and have worn the same tights and baggy top to cover my stomach all week. I have become obsessed with checking my phone to the point where it is psychotic. I have created and airbrushed so many stories in my mind about people that I can't work out which ones to believe. My self-worth is leaking out of me by the minute. My life is one big feral matted dreadlock; I can't even begin to work out how to untangle it and couldn't buy a bottle of conditioner big enough to comb it out.

I wake up and try pulling myself out of my stagnant muddy puddle by making some beauty appointments, and booking Albert in for a dinner date. I need to hang my obsessive mind in the cloakroom and go off and have a day without it.

First stop: nails. I choose black nail polish, and am placed in a row of women with my feet in a spa.

'What can I get you to drink?' my manicurist asks.

'You *haaave* to have the strawberry champagne. It's so good, right?' says the girl next to me, who loudly crunches on boiled sweets from a packet at the same pace one would eat chips.

She ticks every box on the Hollywood checklist: a head that is too big for her body, a little dog in her bag, fluorescent white teeth, glazed eyes, bleached hair and a fake tan. I wonder whether I could get away with taking a photo of her with my phone.

'Um, just water is fine, thank you,' I say.

Next stop: the hairdresser. She bleaches my dark regrowth but says she can't tighten my hair extensions because she doesn't use the same method as they do in Australia. On one of the trips back from the basin, I check my phone and see a missed call from my manager. I listen to the message: the network want to see me for a 'chemistry test' with the male lead who has already been cast in the television pilot. What? I have never heard of a chemistry test; does it mean I'll have to pash him at the end of the toilet-cubicle scene?

I pay at the counter, leave the salon and get a few steps down the street when I hear: 'Excuse me.' It is the hairdresser.

'Uh, yes?'

'Did I do something wrong?' she asks.

'Wrong, no, why?'

'Are you, like, not happy with your hair?'

'No, I love it, you did a great job. Why?'

'You didn't tip. Which is fine, I was only wondering if I had done something to offend you.' She has sleeve tattoos, jet-black hair, bright red lipstick and pale snow-white skin. She scares me.

'Oh god, no, you didn't offend me. I just had no idea you're expected to tip hairdressers here. I'm Australian. I didn't know, I'm so sorry,' I say, fumbling around in my bag for my purse.

'I didn't come out trying to chase a tip — I wanted to make sure you were happy.'

'Here, I'm sorry.' I hand her a twenty-dollar note.

'No, it's okay.'

'Really, I insist.' I put the note in her hand and walk as fast as I can to my car. I am oil and this city is vinegar. You can stir us together and momentarily we look amalgamated, but once things settle we separate again.

We walk into a secret restaurant in the Hollywood Hills and Albert is greeted with a hug from the owner. It feels like we have been allowed into someone's childhood dream world. The lighting is dim and every table is privately sectioned off with delicate and colourful Indian wall hangings, like little individual cubby houses. When we are seated in our hidey-hole for the evening, our waiter brings us a bottle of white wine, bread and olive oil.

'Are you okay?' Albert asks.

I shrug.

'Is it because you aren't on a job at the moment?'

'Yeah, I guess that's a part of it. In between jobs I always seem to fall apart. I am so used to having a script dictate the drama that goes on in my life. When I'm not working and there's no script, it's like my life is on pause and I am forgotten about, like a doll put back into the toy box with the lid closed. It gets pretty dark in there.'

'In order to survive in this industry, you need to be able to change your attitude to your downtime.'

'Yeah, I know. I just wish there wasn't any downtime. I want to live job to job and just rub out the in-between.'

'Rub out your own life? Your own personal script?'

'Yeah, maybe.'

Small plates of tapas continue to arrive from the kitchen: olives, baked cheese and now prawns. I love that we weren't even shown a menu.

'So what brought you out here in the first place?'

'Um, my boyfriend proposed to me.'

'That's lovely. Congratulations.'

'Yeah, it was lovely. He came home from work one day with wet hair and couldn't look at me. He told me to get my cossies and goggles, and we drove to a little bay. I had no idea what was happening. He led me into the water, told me to take a deep breath and follow him. We swam down to the bottom of the sea and he frantically brushed some sand away to reveal the words *Will you be my wife?* written in white rocks.'

'What was your reply?'

'I said I didn't know if I could marry him.'

'Why not?'

'I actually still don't really know. I just wasn't totally sure. When I'm with Tobey I think I'm sure, but then I get an acting job and I get so swept away. There is this particularly powerful feeling of possibility when I'm acting, especially opposite a love interest, and maybe I might miss out on all of that if I were married.'

'How?'

'I feel like I need to keep myself like a blank canvas to be able to transform into a role.'

'So you're willing to sacrifice your own personal life and happiness for your career?'

'I actually don't know how I feel — maybe I'm just scared, maybe that's why I couldn't say yes.'

'What about Tobey? Are you in love with him?'

'Yes,' I say without even realising it and ambitiously put a whole stuffed mushroom in my mouth.

'What are you really chasing with acting?'

'Well, that's a good question, because often I don't even like acting,' I say with my mouth full. 'Sometimes I think I just fell into it to escape monotony. I've always been so scared of having a boring life. Every time I feel routine creeping in, I have to shatter it.'

'There has to be another reason.'

'Um, I've always had this unnatural need to be seen, like I'm invisible or something. Which I guess comes down to wanting people to love me more.'

'It sounds like you are very loved to me. One thing I do know is that fame catapults you in the opposite direction. Most of the famous people in this city are among the loneliest on the planet.'

'I have heard that. Some days I just want to live in a cul-de-sac with a big pregnant belly, and other times I want the freedom to solely chase my career.'

'Is Tobey involved in the cul-de-sac vision?'

'Yeah, he is, but things didn't end well with him and we aren't really speaking now. He broke it off when I was unsure about marriage. He said unless we were both heading in that direction, there wasn't any point in staying together. I didn't want us to break up, and I didn't say a definite "no" to marriage. I just told him I needed time.'

'Do you miss him now?'

'Yeah. But what I do know is things weren't one hundred per cent, so if I said yes, then all those itches would have turned into bigger itches, which would eventually get infected. I don't want an infected marriage. Were you one hundred per cent when you married Pearl?'

'I don't think love is something that can be measured. I knew with every part of me that I wanted to spend the rest of my life with her. Of course she had her broken bits, but so does everyone.'

'How did you deal with those broken bits?'

'The broken bits were a big part of my love for her. Those bits made me love her even more.'

Later the waiter brings us out a chocolate cake to share for dessert. I watch Albert, as he carefully, without blinking, cuts our little round cake into perfect halves.

'Sunday Triggs.' Open sesame, the boom gate goes up. Again I make my way to building C2, and as I walk in the door I run into Shelly, a Sydney actress, who is here for a general meeting. We were never really friends, but we give each other a long hug, just because everything is amplified in America. I tell her I have no idea how long I will take, but she insists on waiting for me at the café next door, so we can have a coffee together when I am finished. She has loneliness written all over her face.

I am plonked down on the single chair in the hallway and the suits stream in past me. Part of me is stupidly calm, and the other part of me is screaming so loudly it is deafening. A scruffy guy walks around the corner. I instantly recognise his face from a television series I watched growing up. As he walks towards me he seems like a moving hologram of himself. I look at him and feel I know him really well. Does everyone feel that way when they see him? Is that what star quality is?

'G'day,' he says in a bad Australian accent.

'G'day,' I reply in a perfect Australian accent.

'You must be Sunny. I'm Sam.' He extends his hand.

I shake it and for some reason am stuck in my chair. I should have stood up as soon as he stopped next to me. If I get up now it will be weird.

'I heard you did really well in your test.' He has a twitch: a small, subtle, quick head nod.

'Really?'

'Yeah, really.'

Awkward, it's awkward: there is no chemistry and he thinks I am a foreign freak.

'Well, I'll see you in there.' He leaves and walks into the theatrette.

I put Listerine strip after Listerine strip on my tongue and hope they don't make us kiss.

Uh-oh. Wild-horse mind has broken loose again. This time it is really dangerous: everyone run for cover; no one is safe. I want to run for cover myself. I hate it here. I hate this fake world where everyone is sugar-coated and no one is ever honest. Why don't I just leave? I'll get up out of my chair, run to the car, go back to the house and get all my stuff packed, and go straight to the airport and wait there for a flight home.

'We're ready for you,' red-hair says.

I walk in and am placed in a chair opposite Sam. Holy shitbags.

Sam opens with: 'So, how do you like LA?'

I hate it; I considered running away just now.

'Yeah, it's great.'

Lie.

'What do you think is great about it?'

Nothing.

'Um, Runyon Canyon is pretty great. I was there yesterday.'

Boring, boring, I am so boring. Runyon Canyon is like being in hell. There is brown dust as far as the eye can see and it stinks of dog poo. I can feel thirty thirsty sets of eyes burning into me, looking for some iota of chemistry, and there is not one drop.

'Oh yeah, did you have a good hike?'

'Yeah I did, but something embarrassing happened.'

Oh my god, I am not about to tell this story.

'Yeah? What?' he asks.

Too late, I have jumped off the cliff; there is no turning back.

'Well, there's no toilets there, and my whole walk I was busting to pee. There was barely anyone around, so I went behind a sparse-looking bush. I was almost finished when two guys and their dogs walked past.'

'Did they see you?'

'I thought I was safe, but it had trickled down through the dust and one of the guys almost stepped in it.'

'Did he see you squatting?' Sam asks, genuinely laughing.

'Yes. Then he gave me a look as if I was the filthiest human being he had ever seen!'

'Noooo!'

We both laugh and I realise we are the only two laughing. I look up and not one of the suits is even smiling. Oh god, stupid, stupid idiot, why on earth did I tell that story? If I had made a dash for it earlier I wouldn't be here in this room wanting to kill myself. In telling that story I was hoping for rapturous laughter and to be instantly crowned the brave, offbeat comedy queen, but instead I look like a dirty freak.

'Okay, let's start the scene, shall we?' red-hair suggests.

'Oh, and we'd like you to lose the accent for this read.'

'Lose the American accent?' I ask.

'No, lose your Australian accent.'

Damn.

Sam winks at me and we read the cocaine scene, without him taking his eyes off the page. Finally it ends (without a pash) and I am released.

Once I am out of the building I start running. I run until I reach my car. When I am safely inside I put my head on the steering wheel.

Oh shit. I forgot about poor Shelly waiting for me at the café. I consider driving off, but I know I would feel too guilty, and don't have her number. I scamper back past the scene of the crime and into the café.

Shelly gives me another extra-long hug. We cover the basics, and I tell her about my disastrous chemistry test.

'I'm sure it wasn't that bad. I'm sure they thought your story was funny; so what if you couldn't actually hear them laughing.'

'It's very sweet of you to try and reassure me, but I promise you —'

Oh shit. Sam has just walked in. Our eyes meet. I instantly look away and try to carry on my conversation with Shelly. He orders something at the counter and makes his way over to us.

'Hey,' he says.

'Hi. I'm so sorry about that,' I reply in a high-pitched voice.

'Sorry for what?'

'For my stupid, unfunny story. I was so nervous and I didn't mean to —'

'It was great. I thought it was funny. Those tests are so

inhumane. I'm Sam by the way.' He goes to shake Shelly's hand.

'Oh, sorry, this is my friend Shelly. Do you want to sit down?'

Please say no.

'Sure, while I wait for my coffee.'

The conversation continues awkwardly, and I am relieved when Shelly launches into a monologue about herself. Wow, she really is a bit of a loser. I stare at my shoes and wish I were invisible.

'So, do you guys know many people here?' Sam asks.

'Not really,' I reply and look back at my feet.

'Do you want to come along and watch one of the worst movies you will ever see tonight? It's a rip-off of *You've Got Mail*. You've seen that one — you know how shit it is, right?'

'Yeah, I've seen it,' I reply.

'Well, this is literally ten times worse.'

'Wow, you're really selling it to me — and I would want to come, why?' I ask.

'Well, I play a copy of the Tom Hanks part and it's opening at the Chinese Theatre tonight, and it could be, I dunno, a kinda cool experience for some gals from the outback who are new in town.'

'Oh no, I can't. I have a meeting with my manager, damn!' Shelly says.

Phew.

'I'll come,' I say.

'Cool. I have to do all the red-carpet bullshit and I can't bear to sit through the film again, but I'll go to the afterparty. Do you want to bring a friend or boyfriend along?'

'Yeah, I'll bring a friend,' I say as the waitress comes over and hands him a takeaway coffee.

He smiles at her. He looks like he hasn't slept for days, and has a sadness in his eyes that doesn't match his Hollywood jawline.

We exchange numbers and he says he will leave the tickets for me at 'Will Call'. I listen to another one of Shelly's monologues and then make an excuse to get out of there.

As I walk to the car I try calling Nina, who doesn't answer. I decide to drive to her place, and stop off on the way to get a bunch of peace lilies. I knock on her door, no answer. I sit on the steps of her apartment and wait and wait.

I start cleaning out my text-message inbox and halfway through I hit one from Tobey:

Damn I adore you Sunday.

He and my mum are the only two people that call me by my full name. I imagine someone else hearing his first word in the morning and it gives me a shiver.

I look up and finally see Nina's car parking in front of me.

'I'm so sorry. I am an awful friend,' I say as she walks towards me.

'It's okay. So am I.'

'Do you want to do something fun tonight?'

'I have to work.'

'Can you chuck a sickie?'

We collect our tickets and make our way up the red carpet. A block of Hollywood Boulevard has been closed off and there is a sea of photographers. The strobing light from the camera flashes is blinding; I would hate to think how bad it would be if the cameras were actually pointing at me. I spot Sam answering questions, and all of a sudden my outfit and bag feel very cheap and very wrong. I feel incredibly unfamous, like the cousin from out of town, and walk as fast as I can to get inside.

We head to the candy bar and Nina orders popcorn. She goes to pay, finds out it is all free, so adds a bag of Hershey's Kisses, a bag of Reese's Pieces and two drinks.

As the lights go down in the cinema there is wild applause. There is squealing, wolf whistles and cheering every time a new character comes on the screen. It is like being at a sporting match, or a pantomime with audience participation. There is something I love about this level of enthusiasm. I have never seen anything like it; Australian premieres are usually dead silent, with some light clapping once the credits come up.

We make our way to the afterparty and are handed some sort of pink-grapefruit Cosmopolitans as we walk in. The room at the Four Seasons is decorated with stilettos, presumably because the lead female character has a shoe fetish and owns a shoe store, which Sam's character tries to put out of business. There are stilettos hanging from the ceiling and lined up on the walls to make you feel like you are inside one giant shoe closet.

I can't understand why women spend huge amounts of money on them. I have no interest in them whatsoever; they're painful, and all they do is slow you down. Somehow I've made it through life without ever owning a pair of stilettos, which Tobey always thought was very cool. Nina took me along to Jimmy Choo's soon after I arrived and I might as well have been in a shop that sold car mufflers. I ended up waiting outside.

'What did you ladies think of the film?'

Uh-oh, two big nerds have appeared. They are both chubby and wear light-blue jeans.

'Yeah it was good,' I say. I clock Nina's expression, which says 'lose them'.

'Where are you girls from?' asks Harry Highpants.

'Australia,' Nina says, literally turning her back on them.

'I've always wanted to go to Australia,' says the other one who wears a colourful, festive shirt.

'Did you like the film?' I ask.

'Yeah, it's a great film. We both worked on it. We're in the accounts department.' He goes on and on in a one-note voice that sounds like white noise.

Both Nina and I wait for a pause where we can duck out. There are no pauses. I scan the room for Sam, who is wearing a faded maroon shirt. I spot him and he looks like he's engrossed in an important conversation.

'Excuse me, I have to use the bathroom. Sunny?' Nina looks at me expectantly.

'Um, yeah, I need to go as well.'

We abandon them mid-sentence.

'We need to be surgical with our time. Better to cut them off early before they get too attached,' Nina says.

'They were only trying to be friendly.'

'Here is not the place to be doing charity work.'

We emerge from the bathroom and accept another pink drink from a ridiculously good-looking waitress. I catch Sam's eye, and he signals for us to come and join him. He is sitting at a table with three other men. One of them, James, is a friend of Sam's, and the other two in suits are the executive producers.

Sam asks me what I thought of the film. I tell him I thought he did very well, and he says that is a very good answer and winks at me. One of the producers starts recounting a story in a voice that is loud and greedy. Sam turns to me so no one else can see him and rolls his eyes, then makes a gun shape with his hand, points it at the roof of his mouth and pretends to pull the trigger.

'So, is it common in Australia to see women squatting on the street?' he asks me quietly.

'Yeah, yeah. You see them everywhere, in gutters, parks. When you've gotta go, you've gotta go.'

He laughs, and brushes his fringe out of his eyes.

I spot a tattoo across his wrist. In black running writing are the letters *KPTOW*.

'What do the letters stand for?' I ask.

'Keep passing the open windows.'

'What does that mean?'

'It's from one of my favourite books. It's the family's

way of telling each other to persevere when things aren't going well.'

'What happens?'

'In the end one of the daughters forgets about the mantra and jumps out a window.'

'Why do you have it tattooed across your wrist?'

'So I won't forget.'

'I wrote *No Smoking* on my hand every morning for almost a month and it worked. I gave up,' I say.

'Really?'

'Yeah, pretty much. Someone told me the Dalai Lama is a sometime smoker, so I don't feel too bad if I have the occasional one when I'm feeling out of my depth.'

'Maybe that needs to be my next tattoo.'

'Do you smoke?'

'Oh, yeah.'

'Then it seriously should be. It works. You could just get *NS*. It would save you writing it on every morning — and it wouldn't smudge. I looked like a grubby schoolgirl for a month.'

I look over and see Nina talking to James; she is animated and I can tell she is considering him as an option.

Sam stands and motions for me to do the same. He excuses us and we move towards the bar with Nina and James following close behind. Nearly everyone around us seems to be staring at Sam, which he is completely oblivious to. He gets a soda water for himself and a whiskey for James, and Nina and I get more sugary cocktails.

The 'wow, this is an exciting life' twinkling alcohol hologram appears and sits in the middle of my chest. I glide into the gear of the person I want to be and all the right words and gestures suddenly become available to me.

'Crazy in Love' by Beyoncé comes on loudly over the sound system. Nina and I look at each other expectantly, and hit the dance floor. It is packed and we dance like teenagers who have escaped out of their bedroom windows and need to get their money's worth before their parents discover them and drag them home. We jump for an entire song, which catches on, and soon we have the whole dance floor jumping.

'How's it going with your new boyfriend?' I scream over the music in Nina's ear.

'Good, how's yours?' she asks and I laugh.

Nina has an innate ability to dance. She is inside the music and her moves look pre-choreographed. I have a wave of jealousy, then come up with the perfect solution: to mimic her. Now we are the two best dancers on the dance floor. I am drenched in sweat, but the hits just keep coming. I see Sam making his way towards us. My first reaction is to stop dancing, but decide that it would be even more embarrassing if I just suddenly stop still. He leans right into me so he can be heard over the music.

'You okay?' he asks, with quite a pronounced head twitch.

'Yeah. Are you okay?'

'Yeah. I've kinda had enough, am thinking of calling it a night. I've got a room upstairs, so I think I'm going to head on up pretty soon. Are you okay to get home?'

'Yeah, I think so. I've got my car here but I don't think I should drive. I had the valet park it when I arrived. Will it be okay if it stays here overnight?'

'Do you want to stay here overnight, too?'

'Um …'

Stay with him?

'I'll organise you two a room. Just go to reception and tell them your name once you are finished up here.'

'Oh okay, great. Thank you.'

'Thanks for coming,' he says, and gives me a sibling-type peck on the cheek.

Was I ignoring him by coming over here with Nina? Did he get fed up waiting for me and decide to leave?

We continue to dance. James comes over carrying four shots. I shake my head as he offers me one, so he and Nina have two each. He isn't a great dancer and I can tell he is dazzled by Nina's moves. He whispers something in her ear, and she laughs loudly. The next time I look at them they are pashing. They start getting out of control and I decide to leave them to it.

I head back to the bar to get a glass of water and start feeling over it all and ready for bed. Do I have to stay here? Can I just leave or has he already booked it? It probably costs a bloody fortune; rich people always assume everyone else is as rich as them. Shit. I decide I better stay.

As I walk out of the function room I am handed a large white paper bag from a woman at the door. Freebies! I take a quick peek inside, before heading to reception.

While the man on the desk is looking me up on his system, I ask if I can fix up the fee now.

'It's all been taken care of. Right this way, ma'am.'

'Do you know what my room number is? I just have to tell my friend.'

I go back to Nina and James, who are still attached

by the mouth. I try to get her attention, but she is drunk and sloshy and in her own world. I take a pen out of my bag and write our room number on her hand while they continue to pash.

I get into my room and it is so beautiful I want to kiss the walls. It is dusty pink and grandma fancy. I have a bubble bath, slide into my crispy new bed for the night and pour out all my new things from the goodie bag. Wow. In Australia you'd be lucky to get a few shampoo and conditioner sachets and a chocolate bar. This one has lipstick (M.A.C!), a watch, two fragrances (his and hers), flash-looking peanut butter, pyjama bottoms, a peace-sign necklace, a teeth-whitening pack, underpants and two vouchers: one for a free cut and colour at a hairdresser in Beverly Hills, and the other one is for two free racks of ribs at a new bar and grill. Woo hoo!

Why am I so obsessed with free stuff? Ever since I can remember I have been. When I was little I used to be more excited about the lolly bags that were given out than the actual birthday parties.

A few hours later I wake to my phone ringing and a very sober-sounding Nina.

'Where are you? Have you left without me?' she asks.

'No, I'm upstairs. My room number is on your hand.'

She comes in carrying her stilettos and three goodie bags, dumps them on the floor and flops onto the bed.

'How did you go?' I ask her.

'Just came from across the hall. Rooted him, of course.'

'Oh my god, are you serious? How was it?'

'Terrible. He was a rammer-homer. He was hard and

fast, and it hurt, and he didn't give a shit about me. Then he dropped straight to sleep and he is the worst jolter ever. He did these huge jolts in his sleep and didn't even wake himself up. Oh, also I didn't like his smell. He smelt like guinea pig.'

'How could you root him if you didn't like his smell?'

'Because I'm a filthy slut, Sunny.'

'You certainly are,' I say, and we drop off to sleep.

Again, my ringing phone wakes me. My mouth tastes like a rat slept in it, and my head is thumping in a very dehydrated way.

'Heo,' comes out of my mouth.

'Sunny, it's Sam. Did I wake you?'

'Um, yeah, you did. You definitely got my first word of the day.' How can it be light already?

'Sorry. Should I let you go?' he says.

'No, no, you're right. What's happening?'

'Was wondering if you guys wanted to grab some breakfast? Did you end up staying here?'

'Yeah, we did. Okay, in, like, fifteen minutes?'

'Sure, see you in the foyer then.'

'Righteo,' I say.

'Right what?'

'Just means "yeah alright".'

'Morning,' I say, feeling like a dirty stopout in last night's dress. At least I'm not in big embarrassing stilettos.

'Hi. Sorry I left so quickly last night,' Sam says with a head twitch.

'No, that's fine. I couldn't wake Nina, she was dead to the world.'

'I tried James's room, but he didn't answer. Was he still there when you left?'

'Yup.'

We walk outside and into some very bright sunshine that requires a pair of sunglasses I do not have. While waiting for the valet to bring Sam's car around, I can't think of anything to say, so I fumble around in my bag, find my Fisherman's Friends and offer Sam one.

'No thanks. I can't stand those things,' he says.

'Oh, can't you? They're my favourite. I brought a few packets over from Australia in case I couldn't get them here.'

Silence. Long silence. Shit.

'You know, when I was growing up I thought you had to be a fisherman to be allowed to buy these. I thought you had to show some sort of certificate at the shops to prove that you really were a fisherman,' I say.

Sam's mouth smiles at me, which his frowning eyebrows don't agree with.

More silence.

'Anyway, that's obviously not the case … Is this your car?' I ask, as the valet finally arrives with a small red car. There is nothing cool about it. It looks cheap and kind of dangerous, like it's too old to be on the road.

'Sure is. Meet Barbarella the rollerskate.'

'Nice to meet you, Barbarella. Wow. I think you're the first person I've met in LA that doesn't have a fancy-pants car.'

'Hey, watch it. Barbie is up there with the best of them in the fancy stakes. I won her in a poker game off a friend who paid ninety dollars for her. He made me promise that I would drive her until her dying day. That was years ago, and she still runs like a dream. I've thought about getting her put down but I don't have the heart.'

I think you can tell a lot about a person by getting into their car when they aren't expecting a passenger. It takes him a good while to clear the bottles, wrappers, scripts and clothes off my seat. I hop in and sit forward, hoping that what looks like melted chocolate on the seat behind me won't stain my dress.

We head to a vegan café in Silver Lake. Sam rolls a cigarette as he drives.

'I hate things like last night,' he says.

'What part of it don't you like?'

'Every bit of it. The shit film, the idiot people that congratulate you on the shit film ...'

'Oh, what a relief. You are the first American I've met that isn't positive. You should come and live in Australia. You would fit in so well there.'

'Maybe I should. Would love to come and check out the squatting-women phenomenon.'

I laugh.

'You have the best laugh,' he says.

'Oh no, I don't, it's so embarrassing. I always think I will get around to taming it one day but I haven't yet.'

'Don't.'

'I won't change it: I will just train myself to do a smaller version of it. So why are you an actor if you hate everything that goes along with it?'

'I'm not going to be for much longer. As you can see I'm going through the process of selling out. I am going to do a few more crap films and maybe another crap television series, if this pilot goes ahead, and then I'm getting out.'

'What will you do then?'

'I'm not sure. Find some hobbies, I guess.' He takes long drags of his rollie. Smoke fills the car.

'Do you have a clothesline?' I ask.

'Why? Do you need to do some laundry?'

'No, it's just I'm doing a survey to find out how many people living in America have clotheslines.'

'No, I don't have one.'

'I haven't met one person here that has one. Seems so odd because saving the planet is what's so "in" here at the moment.'

'That's LA for you.' He checks his watch. 'Damn, I can never manage to get there on time.' Another head twitch.

'Did you make a booking for brekkie?'

'Brekkie meaning breakfast?'

'Yeah.'

'That's cool. I'm going to use that from now on. No, no booking, but we're meeting a few of my friends for "Silent Saturday brekkie".'

'What do you mean? Why silent?'

'We meet every Saturday at the same café and don't speak to each other. You are only allowed to speak to the waitress when you order.'

'Why? I don't get it.'

'So we can all just read the paper and not feel guilty about it. We used to meet every week — and it was basically silent anyways. Everyone is usually exhausted on Saturday mornings and all you really want to do is be quiet and read the paper, so bringing in the silent rule takes the pressure off having to make conversation.'

'How am I going to ask people if they have a clothesline?'

We walk from the car to the café and I spot a quarter on the ground. Without thinking I squat down and pick it up.

'You are so sweet,' he says, smiling in a slightly patronising, slightly surprised way.

'What? Are you rich enough not to pick up a quarter off the ground?'

'Yes, I am.'

'Do you ever have to work again?'

'Not if I don't want to.'

'How did you make your money?'

'From a television show, whose name we do not mention.'

'Right, I know the one.'

No point in lying and saying I didn't.

'Did you get it in Australia?'

'Yeah. That's why I was so nervous when I first met you.'

An older hippyish couple are already there and wave to us as we enter, then a woman arrives with her young son. She tells the waitress her son only eats white things, so he will have a plate of anything in the kitchen that is white. He is an unusual-looking little boy, who seems to walk only on his tiptoes.

Sam points to the buckwheat berry pancakes on the menu, then does a charade-type mime to illustrate how good they are and that I must order them. I watch him as he goes under our table with a pile of napkins and props them under one of the legs, to stop it from being wobbly. Isn't he too famous to do that?

Two more guys arrive separately when we are halfway through our meal. One looks like an ex-junkie with a pilling jumper, and the other one looks like a big, licky puppy dog, but with a tattoo of tree roots snaking up his neck.

We eat in silence, and I can't stop smiling. I feel like I am in the lead-up to someone's surprise party. Once we are all finished Sam goes up to the register and pays the bill. Again he gives me a slightly patronising smile when I try to hand him a twenty-dollar note.

We drive back to the Four Seasons to get my car, and I make sure I'm not the one that breaks the silence.

'It's good, right?' he says.

'Yeah,' I smile. 'I did Vipassana a few years ago, which is a ten-day silent retreat. I found it so hard to start speaking again once it was over. I realised how much crap I spoke day to day. I just make noise to fill in space.'

'Was it hard?'

'No, it was easy. It was the happiest ten days of my life.'

'Wow, that sounds freaky, I could never do that.'

'What's freaky about it?'

'I wouldn't trust myself, I'd lose it. Did anyone lose it when you did it?'

'One guy did actually try to kill himself and got taken away in an ambulance.'

'Are you serious?'

'Yeah. Whatever's there will come out. You sit and meditate in four-hour blocks. You can't hide from anything.'

'Shit. So what about you? Do you want to act for the rest of your life? I mean you should, you're great, but is that what you want to do?'

'Um, I don't really know. When I'm actually doing it and I'm underwater and it's quiet and the world ceases to exist then, yes, it is what I want to do.'

'But?'

'But I guess the majority of my life is on the surface where it's noisy. I spend my time faffing around getting hair extensions and trying to get acting jobs, and trying to convince myself that I am a worthwhile person even if I do fall under the title of "unemployed".'

'Have you got hair extensions?'

'Yep,' I answer, feeling like an idiot Barbie doll.

'Why?'

'To make myself prettier, I guess.'

'Whether you had a shaved head or double the hair, you'd still be beautiful.'

'That's a nice thing to say, thank you.'

'I know what you mean about that whole underwater feeling. I have only ever experienced it once.'

'When was that?'

'It was on a little indie film that never got released.'

'Is that the only time?'

'Pretty much, yeah.'

'But you've had so much work.'

'Yeah, but all the that work is noisier than my normal life.'

As we drive along I look up at the Hollywood sign and think of the actress who committed suicide by jumping off the letter 'H'. Was her life too noisy? I wonder whether it was lack of control over her fate in this industry that made her do it. Maybe she was bursting at the seams with creativity and never given an outlet. Did she feel like she had rehearsed her whole life — giving out free samples here and there — for a performance that would never actually be seen?

That evening I take Albert to the new bar and grill to use the voucher from the freebie bag. I can see why they are trying to get people in: it is relatively empty and, even though it has been fitted out well, it has a bleak, sterile atmosphere.

We order a full rack of ribs each, chips and a salad. As the waitress takes our order I wonder if she thinks we're on a date. I hope she thinks he's my dad instead.

I tell Albert all about Sam's premiere.

'Why am I telling you? I'm sure you've been to so many openings of your own films. Can you tell me about these movies you've written?'

'Oh, nothing really to tell, my dear — they're all quite silly.'

'Are they comedies?'

'Yes, mostly romantic comedies.'

I love the way Albert tries to wriggle out of talking about himself — it's so un-American.

'Are there any that you're proud of?'

'No, not really. I wrote for one of the big studios and they basically outlined what they wanted with each script. The movies that were made were never really my own.'

I check my phone.

'Are you waiting for a call?' he asks.

'No, just checking the time. The food seems to be taking a while.'

'It hasn't been too long.'

'Oh. Sorry, I'm really impatient. Actually I'm not impatient, I just think life goes too slowly.' Albert laughs. 'Even when I was young I would stare at the clock, and try to will the hands to hurry up. I remember the first time I ever cooked a cake I doubled the temperature of the oven, thinking it would cook the cake in half the time.'

'Have things sped up as you've gotten older?'

'Nup. I still wish time away,' I say as half a pig's ribcage gets laid out in front of me.

The waitress puts a big white bib on me, then one on Albert. The ribs smell synthetic and sweet.

I watch Albert as he slices a rib off and starts eating it with his fingers. I push my plate forward slightly.

'Everything alright?' Albert asks.

'Um, I don't think I can do this. Even though I sometimes eat meat now, I was brought up a vegetarian and I've never eaten ribs before.'

'They're very good.'

'I'm sure they are but I just can't eat them, sorry. Will you be able to eat some of mine, too?' I ask.

'I'll be lucky to get through my own.'

I catch the waitress's eye and explain to her that I no longer want the ribs, but also tell her I haven't touched them and ask if she can offer them to someone in the kitchen. I don't want this pig to have died for no reason. I apologise again to Albert for being such a pain and with my bib still on I get started on the salad and chips.

As Albert rolls his eyes, and at the same time tries to hold back a smile, I can tell he would have made a good father.

'I got a text from Sam inviting us to a party tonight,' I say on the phone to Nina the next morning.

'Count me out. I have just started on this new ballerina tea from my Chinese doctor. I can't stop shitting. It is amazing; it's better than laxatives and without the cramping. You should try it — I have heaps.'

'No thanks.'

'Where's the party?' she asks.

'Beverly Hills.'

'House or bar?'

'House.'

'Could be a famous party. Okay, if things calm down by this afternoon we'll go.'

We are handed glasses of champagne as we walk into the party, which is packed, dark and loud. The ceilings are high, and the house itself is magnificent. There is a bar full of staff wearing white, and the air smells like perfume and possibility. The house opens out onto a massive garden with a pool that looks like a lake. There is a jazz band playing under a silver marquee, and white origami birds and lanterns have been hung through the trees.

'G'day, Australia!' I turn around as Sam and James the guinea pig come up behind us.

'You didn't tell me it was fancy dress. I love fancy dress!' I say as they both kiss us.

'It's not,' Sam replies.

'What about that girl?' I say, pointing to a blonde woman covered in henna tattoos, wearing a bright orange sari and Indian jewellery.

'Oh, that's Ria. She recently got back from India and she's obsessed,' Sam says, taking a sip from his bottle of mineral water.

'What about him?' I ask, pointing to a man wearing a long skirt and an open suit jacket showing a bare chest, draped with thick gold chains.

'He's just a freak,' the guinea pig says.

People are bursting with colour, ambition and appetite. Everywhere you look there is uncensored, unapologetic freedom of expression. The room is filled with bodies that are anorexic, obese, black, white, young and old, with the common denominator being success.

Sam introduces us to a man beside him. I have met him before somewhere, or I recognise him from a film I have seen. Yes! A comedy, I think it was. I instantly get nervous, but Nina is amazingly calm and chatty.

You can take her anywhere; she makes friends with everyone so quickly. Does that mean she's built for this industry and I'm not? I have never been the class clown, and have always been quite quiet. I'm okay one on one, but in a group I seem to fade in colour. My worst fear is not tall buildings or sharks but being put on the spot;

getting picked out of a crowd and asked to tell the audience something about myself. I wonder if a shy actor is the same as a pilot with a fear of flying. Maybe that's why I do it: because it terrifies me.

This party is like opening the cover of a tabloid magazine. I'm being introduced to people and knowing their names before they are said. Not just actors, but musicians, directors, models and even an Olympian. A tray of sushi passes us — my favourite — but for some reason I don't feel as though I can eat in front of Sam. I should be joining in on the conversation, but every time I go to say something it goes past a harsh judging panel in my mind and nothing is deemed good enough to actually make it out of my mouth. Is this city slowly erasing me?

I excuse myself, grab some eel sushi and two fancy fruit skewers, and escape to the bathroom. I sit on the toilet with the lid down and eat. I know this is unhygienic, but the bathroom is so spotless and lovely and quiet. I decide to clean out my handbag. I put wrappers, napkins and a half-eaten packet of dried fruit in the bin, and make piles of receipts on the sink that I can keep for tax purposes. I look at my profile in the mirror and wonder if I should get a nose job. Would it change the course of my life? My nose has often been referred to as 'prominent'.

There is a knock at the door. Oops, I have been in here for an unusually long time.

'Won't be a sec!' I collect up all my receipts and quickly use the toilet. As I'm washing my hands, there is a second, louder knock. I open the door and see Nina standing in front of me with a very worried look on her face. She dashes past me and slams the door.

'Are you okay?' I ask through the door.

'No!'

'Sunny! Come and meet the host!' Sam yells out from behind me.

Oh my god. The 'host' is one of the most famous actresses in America. Oh my fucking god. I know about her latest break-up, I know what her dog looks like, I know what she orders at Starbucks, I know what diet she's on, I know too much. I am a voyeur. Will she know how much I know? Even if I didn't intentionally dig out this information, how could I miss the glaring headlines on the front of magazines while waiting in the queue at the grocery store?

She is golden. She looks like an Oscar. She reaches out to shake my hand. We shake and, uh-oh, my hand is wet.

'Lovely to meet you and sorry about my wet hand. I just came out of the bathroom. It's not, like, creepy wet. I just washed it,' I say.

Sam cracks up laughing.

'Are we out of hand towels?' she asks, releasing that signature multimillion-dollar smile.

I think we could actually be really good friends.

'No, I just thought they were too pretty to use, and I had to leave the bathroom really quickly because someone was banging on the door …'

Somebody save me before I tell her I think my friend might have her diarrhoea back because she drank too much ballerina tea.

'Have you got a clothesline?' Sam asks her, with a wink to me.

'Uh, no. Why?'

'Sunny is obsessed with clotheslines,' he replies.

'Oh.' She smiles again, then is whisked away, probably much to her relief, away from the oddball Australian.

'Sorry,' I say to Sam. 'I am such an embarrassing friend for you to have brought along. Why does everything suddenly become wee-related when I am around you? The wee story when we were doing the chemistry test, and now not drying my hands properly after weeing.'

More people appear beside us: two insanely stunning girls. How? How can people be this good-looking? They hug Sam and I slip away and get back to Nina in the toilet.

I knock on the door.

'No!' she calls out urgently.

'Nina, it's me, Sun.'

After a moment she lets me in.

'I've shat myself,' she says and I burst out laughing.

'Don't laugh! It happened when I was talking to a big sort, and I had to run off!'

'It's fine, it's fine, we'll just sneak away.'

'No, it's not fine,' she says as she dashes for the toilet.

There is a loud farting noise and I get the giggles again. I put my hands over my mouth.

'Shut up, you mole!' she says.

'I'm so sorry, I can't help it!'

There is a knock at the door and we both freeze. Nina looks utterly mortified.

'Just a minute!' I yell out.

'No, no, no! I can't leave!' Nina says.

I grab a pile of the embroidered linen hand towels and tell her to shove them down her pants. I spray too much air freshener, flush the toilet, grab her hand and lead her out and to the car.

As I am about to drive off I notice she is crying. I go to give her a hug.

'Don't touch me. I'm revolting. I'm such a fuck-up,' she says.

'What? You are not a fuck-up. It was just a silly little accident that we'll laugh about tomorrow.'

'No, not only this. What am I doing? I'm so obsessed with weight loss and food. Alcoholics can stop drinking altogether, but I have to deal with my enemy on a daily basis. I can't escape it.'

'What about going back to one of those support groups?'

'No, they just make me worse. I get ideas when people share their stories. Tips on the easiest foods to bring back up and the best diet pills.'

I pass her a tissue. 'Let's get out of here,' I say.

As we drive away my phone rings.

'Hello?'

'Hey, it's Sam.'

'Hi, Sam.'

'Where are you?'

Nina shakes her head.

'We're in the car. We had to leave. Nina isn't very well.'

Nina's head-shaking becomes more vigorous.

'Is she okay?' he asks.

'Yeah, she will be.'

'Are you going to come back?'

'No, I don't think I will, Sam, but thanks for inviting us. I have to go because I'm driving.'

'Can't you talk and drive at the same time?'

'Yeah, but I don't want to get arrested.'

'Why would you get arrested?'

'Oh yeah, I forgot it's legal here. It's illegal in Australia
— and so it should be. It's really dangerous. I better go.'

'Bye.'

'Bye.' I hang up.

'He wants to stick it in,' Nina says.

'No, he doesn't. He thinks I'm a weirdo.'

'You're wrong. I can tell by the way he looks at you.'

'Hey, something I noticed tonight: James the guinea
pig kind of has a big bum.'

'Ah! No! Please, no! Are you sure? There is nothing
worse. Smelling like a guinea pig is nothing compared to
having a big arse.'

'It's not massive but it's noticeably big for his frame.'

'How could I not have noticed? Guess I was pretty
pissed that night.'

I put Nina's party clothes in a bucket to soak while she
has a shower, then run a bath with lavender and orange
oil. I make us peppermint teas, and sit down on the floor
cross-legged next to the bath.

'So, went off the antidepressants, as you can probably
tell,' Nina says.

'How come?'

'One of the main reasons I went on them was because
I thought they might help me stop bingeing, but they
didn't at all.'

'I'm so glad you've gone off them, Nina. I really think
you have to deal with things as they happen in life, like
doing the washing-up as you go along. You don't want to
end up with a huge pile of dirty dishes with dried bits of
food all over them that are impossible to get off.'

'I know you think I've changed but I haven't really. It's just hard going without acting work for so long.'

'I know you haven't really changed, but I do think you need to get out of here.'

'What, and go back to Sydney?'

'Yep. I think it's time. I don't think this city brings out the best in you.'

'I've actually been thinking about that but I don't know if I can. What will I tell people? "Hi, yeah, I'm great! Haven't worked in three years."'

'No one cares, Nina! People only care about themselves. You'll get work at home, and you can live by the sea. You always said you would go mad if you didn't live by the sea.'

'And I have gone mad, haven't I?'

'A bit, but I still love you.'

I wake up in Nina's bed. She tells me she is feeling much better. She tries to talk me into having a protein shake for breakfast, but I talk her into avocado and sardines on chunky rye toast. Then Nina takes me out to see some sights.

First up: Fred Segal, a clothing store that provides one-stop shopping for celebrities and stylists. They house the world's best designers under one roof, and my god do you pay for the 'convenience'.

'Get on the blower and get Tobey back before he shacks up with this girl. That's my opinion,' she yells from the change room next door after I've filled her in about Tobey.

I go and sit on the chair in her change room with a stupidly expensive dress on.

'Why didn't I say "yes" there and then when he asked me to marry him? That's my problem: as soon as I feel like something is out of my reach I immediately want it more.'

'You just needed this girl to come along to give you a little wake-up call. Tobey is the catch of the century, Sun. He's hot, he isn't in this industry, and he owns his own business. He'll be snatched up any second. I can see why you want to test the waters, but guys like George and Sam will never settle down. They will still be playing the field when they're dirty old men. I mean go shag them, go crazy, but at the end of the day you want to stay away from guys like that. Trust me. As if you want to end up like me, the good-time girl. It's no life. It's like a game of musical chairs, and when the music stops you want to get that chair.'

'I don't get that analogy.'

'You don't want the music to stop and be at the age where you want to have a baby, and have no man on the scene. I have never met anyone that wants a baby as much as you do. I don't want to see you put your career first, then wake up one day and really regret it,' she says.

'Do you think I'd be happy just being a stay-at-home mum that gets the occasional acting job?'

'Success doesn't keep you warm at night. A big filthy sort does.'

We decide we can't afford anything in the store and make our way over to H&M and Forever 21 at the Beverly Center, where we find rip-offs of everything for next to nothing. Then we head to M Café on Melrose Avenue. It's a macrobiotic paradise.

I get a plate of maple-glazed brussels sprouts with scarlet quinoa and a crispy teriyaki seitan steak (pretend meat). Nina orders the Californian club sandwich with tempeh bacon (more pretend meat). The guy on the table next to us has a shirt on that says *I'm not a gynaecologist, but I'll take a look*, which Nina finds hysterically funny.

'I don't think Sam is in that "bad boy, shag you and never call you" category,' I say.

'Oh, yes he is. Trust me, he pioneered that category.'

'I think you're wrong; he's different. I met some friends of his when we went to breakfast and they were really nerdy.'

'What does nerdy friends have to do with anything? Hello, big bum was no dork — he rammed me home and never called.'

'Is it big bum, or guinea pig?'

'Um. What do you think?'

'It's not up to me, he's your boyfriend.'

'Okay, big bum. It makes my skin crawl every time I say it. Big bum, big bum, big bum.'

'Did you talk to him last night?' I ask.

'Nup.'

'Why not?'

'Dunno. He didn't try to talk to me either. That's the way it goes in this town: everyone dates up.'

'What do you mean "dates up"?'

'Everyone tries to date someone better than themselves. Hey, have you heard from George, on the subject of fuckwits?'

'No. It's so weird, huh?'

'So what happened?'

'He came over to help me with an audition, and haven't heard from him since.'

'And did you instigate the kiss?'

'I think so, but only because it was in the script.'

'They're exactly the same those two, you know. An American and an Australian version of the same person. Broody, handsome heartbreakers,' she says as we both go for the last bite of the famous carrot cake. 'Did you know that the principles of macrobiotic food come from traditional oriental medicine?'

'Oh, awesome. Will it give me the runs?' I ask.

Last stop, the Beverly Wilshire for a glass of champagne. I recognise the foyer from the movie *Pretty Woman*.

'Can you take my picture?' I ask.

'No fucking way! Keep walking.'

I force her to, so I can send it to my eldest sister. We had *Pretty Woman* on video; it had been taped off the TV. We watched it so many times it broke.

'Come home to Australia with me. I'll hold your hand really tightly as we land,' I say, picking at the complimentary platter of wasabi peas and smoked almonds.

'I'll think about it.'

Nina goes off to work, and I head home and stare at a blank screen wondering what to write to Tobey. Everything I write sounds clichéd. I finally end up with:

Hi. I think I really need to see you. I looked into getting on a flight home. What do you think I should do?

I wake up to an untitled email from Tobey.

I can't help you decide what to do with your travel plans.

Shit. That is icy cold. I stare at that one sentence on my screen and feel numb, like I have some sort of built-in safety switch that is shutting off my emotions.

I walk down to the house. Damn, Albert is not up yet. I need something or someone to get me out of my head, which feels like it has a ticking time bomb inside it.

I open the cupboard and search for any form of chocolate, but instead come across a sealed packet of Froot Loops. I pour them out onto the kitchen table and start counting. One thousand and sixty, in a packet that weighs three hundred and forty grams, with thirty-eight grams of sugar per one hundred grams. I start sorting them into colour-coded piles. Blue, one hundred and thirty-two and a half; purple, one hundred and forty-five; green, one hundred and thirty-five and a half; yellow, one hundred and thirty-six; orange, two hundred and seventy-six (!); and red, two hundred and thirty-five.

I wonder why there are so many more orange and red ones. Is it purely random? Are they the cheapest to make?

Or maybe there have been studies to show that these are the two most popular flavours.

'Goodness me, what are you doing?' Albert asks as he comes into the kitchen.

'Just keeping busy. Sorry I opened these. I'll buy you a new packet. Would you like some breakfast?'

'What are you suggesting? A bowl of blue ones?'

'I was thinking more along the lines of bacon and eggs.'

'Yes, please.'

I start cooking and have my back to Albert as much as I can, so as to be able to mouth the directions to my imaginary cooking show without him thinking I am a mad person.

'You are such a good mimic,' I say as Albert mimics the morning birdcalls quietly to himself as he reads the paper.

'Not as good as Pearl. She was the queen of bird noises. I'm just copying her.'

'Oh, I wish I could have met her. Tell me something else about her.'

'She used to wear sweatbands on her wrists to the airport while farewelling me, when I went on business. She would cry every time and said the bands were more absorbent than tissues.'

I clear the Froot Loops off the table, and we sit down to a big greasy breakfast.

Later, I crawl back into bed and start working my way through Albert's *Six Feet Under* DVD set on my computer. I try calling Tobey; there is no answer, so

I leave a message asking him to call me. I lose hours watching episode after episode. The phone rings. I press pause; it's a private number. It's him.

'Hello?'

'So are you, like, totally famous in Australia?'

'Sorry, who's this?'

'Sam.'

'Oh, hi. Why are you asking me that?'

'I just googled you and you have your own fan sites.'

I laugh.

'So are you?'

'I wouldn't say I'm totally famous, no.'

'How long have you been acting?'

'About ten years.'

'Do you get recognised on the street?'

'Sometimes. Hey, sorry we left so quickly the other night,' I say, changing the subject.

'That's okay,' he replies, which follows with a silence that is a beat too long.

'What are you up to?'

'You know, kicking around. What are you up to?'

'Just watching DVDs.'

'Hey, are you busy next weekend?'

'Um … No, not really. Why?'

'I'm going to Sundance. My friend has a condo in Salt Lake City that'll be empty. I thought maybe you might like to come along, and watch some films …'

'Oh Sam, that's such a nice offer. God, I don't know …'

'You don't have to decide right now.'

'I've always wanted to go, but um …'

The conversation starts to sound like microwave popcorn when it's ready: long pauses between pops.

'No pressure. I thought I'd ask on the off chance you were free … Have a think about it and let me know.'

'Okay, thanks.'

I have no idea what to do. I call Nina to see what she thinks.

'Shitbags, that's a tough one, Sun. First thing you have to get clear: are you willing to shag him? If he takes you away for the weekend he will definitely expect you to put out.'

'I don't think so; he just likes me. I think he's a bit lonely.'

'He definitely isn't lonely, but I reckon you should go. It would be an amazing experience.'

'Hey, do you reckon Sam has a say in who's cast in this pilot?'

'Gosh, I hadn't thought of that. Yeah, he would have some form of casting approval. Do you think this invitation has something to do with the pilot? Like another call back?'

'I've got no idea.'

We board the plane and I go to put my jacket in the overhead compartment. A stewardess leaps towards me and takes it off to be hung up. I've given away the fact that I have never flown business class before I've even sat down.

'Can I get you two a drink?' she asks while we're waiting for take-off.

'Yes, two champagnes, please,' I say.

'Oh no, not for me. Just a soda,' Sam says.

'Oh, come on, you have to, it's compulsory!'

When we are in the air I insist we both lay our chairs back so we are lying out flat, both with champagne in hand. I can't stop smiling and take up the air hostesses' every offer.

'Look at you,' he says.

'I'm having the best time.'

We decide what to order from the menu.

'I can't believe how much food excites me,' I say.

'You're the opposite to my ex-girlfriend.'

'Wasn't she much of an eater?'

'She was a big eater but she didn't have any taste, like literally no sense of taste.'

'Are you serious? Was she born with no tastebuds?'

'No, she lost her sense of taste after a car accident when she was a teenager.'

'I've never heard of that. What does she eat? Just the cheapest plainest birdseed food she can find?'

'No, she was really big on textures. Her favourite thing was chocolate mousse. She loved anything that had the consistency of clouds. I don't know why I am talking about her like she's dead. She isn't.'

'Did she drink cheap wine?'

Sam laughs. 'It can actually be quite dangerous. People with no taste can eat and drink things that are out of date and not know.'

'Yeah, right. Why did you break up?'

'It was time to,' he says, closing the subject.

'Hey, any word on the TV pilot?' I bravely ask with my champagne courage. 'I haven't heard anything.'

'Look, I think you're a slam dunk for the part, but there are delays with the network. You know how these things go, they can take forever,' he says, closing the subject again.

'What are scallions?' I ask, looking at the menu.

'You don't know what scallions are?'

'No. I have never heard the word scallion. I really like it, though.' God, champagne makes me really like everything.

'They are long, thin green-and-white onions.'

'Oh, spring onions.'

We drink more and more champagne and I make up a song to the tune of 'You say tomayto and I say tomato'.

'You say scallion and I say spring onion / You say to go and I say takeaway / Scallions, spring onions / Take away, to go /

Let's call the whole thing off.'

We continue on the champagne, flick through movies and eat French chocolates out of the box. The 'this is who I really am' twinkling hologram has arrived back in the middle of my chest.

'Hey, would you have invited me along if I was missing the top joint of my little finger?' I ask.

'Yeah.'

'Top two joints?'

'Yeah,' he replies quickly.

'Whole finger?'

'No, I draw the line at chicks with a whole finger missing.' He looks at me suspiciously. 'Show me your hands.'

I do.

'Lucky.'

We land in Salt Lake City. As we step into the airport a group of men run towards us. Some have video cameras and some stills cameras. A few cameras are pointed at me but most of them are on Sam. They ask hungry questions, but Sam stays silent.

He grabs my hand and keeps his head down. I feel like this should be happening in slow motion. I imagine us on the front cover of a crappy magazine, mid-step, hand in hand, with a 'leave us alone, we're just normal human beings' look on our faces.

We are safely shuffled into the back seat of a black SUV. I always thought the American paparazzi would be tanned and toned with flashy white perfect teeth. Oh no. Most of them aren't white, some look like students, and one looks like he's fresh out of jail.

'Animals,' Sam says.

'Why don't you just tell them to piss off?'

'Because as soon as one of us says a word it becomes an exclusive interview, and those low-lifes get themselves ten thousand dollars.'

We drive through a winter wonderland; this place looks like pictures of Santa's village in the North Pole. There are fairy lights in the trees and the snow looks fake, like piles of icing sugar.

'Leroy's a Mormon,' Sam whispers in my ear, referring to our driver, like a scallywag little kid who points out a fat person to his mother in a supermarket. Leroy has a permanent smile on his face, and sings quietly as he drives.

We arrive at our condo, which looks out over a giant ski slope. Sam chooses his bedroom on the second floor and I choose mine on the third. Then he leads me into an underground cellar, which is lined with hundreds of bottles of wine. He selects an armload and instructs me to do the same.

'Are you sure we're allowed? Won't your friend mind?'

'Trust me, he can afford it.'

'I don't know which ones to get.'

'Grab some of those on your right.'

I look at the backs of my hands, then reach up and get two bottles.

'Why did you look at your hands then?' Sam asks.

'I didn't.'

'Don't lie.'

'Um. I don't know my left from my right.'

'Bullshit.'

'As if I'd make up something as embarrassing as that!

My right hand has a freckle on it.'

'You are so gorgeous.'

'As if that's gorgeous. It's not just sometimes, either. I have to check my hands every time.'

'Thank god for that freckle.'

'Well, this is the scary thing: it's fading.' I show him.

'Shit, it is, too,' he says, and cracks up laughing.

We go back upstairs and Sam opens a bottle and goes to pour two glasses.

'Not for me, I can't drink red. It gives me a headache.'

'How can you not drink red? It's from 1982.' He continues to pour the second glass.

'The year I was born,' I say, and he momentarily stops pouring and stares at me, as if I'd just told him I'd done time in jail.

He wouldn't be that much older than me, would he? I guess he would be getting into his late thirties.

He hands me a glass of wine, then presses a button on the wall, which makes the fireplace instantly light up.

'Ahhh!' I clap. 'That's incredible! I have never seen that before. Wow, one button to light the fire.'

'You've never seen an automatic gas fire before? It's really common.'

'Oh. Well, this is my first time in the snow, so maybe that's why.'

Already Sam is topping up his own glass and starts to roll a cigarette.

'Can I have one of those, too?' I ask.

'Are you feeling out of your depth?'

'No, why?'

'You told me you only smoke when you feel out of your depth.'

'Oh yeah, that's right. Maybe I am a little bit,' I say.

He finishes off the bottle and grabs another one for the road.

Leroy drives us into the sunset, and I just cannot believe the vastness of the landscape. Sam reaches into the front and turns the radio up a bit too loud. We drive with the windows down and the heating on full bore. He continues to chain smoke and drinks straight from the bottle.

We arrive at Robert Redford's Sundance Resort. There are fires in drums lining a walkway over little bridges to a small theatre. We settle in to watch a documentary that tells the story of a serial rapist–murderer who is now on death row. He lured women in by hiding in public parks and playing a tape of a child's voice crying out for help. As soon as his victims were near enough he would grab them.

'Did you know what this was about?' I whisper, when we are about ten minutes in.

'Yeah,' Sam says.

I hate this sort of thing; it scares me to my bones.

Finally it ends and we go to a private room in the restaurant called The Tree Room. We are seated on a ridiculously large wooden table, surrounded by Native American art.

'Hi! My name is Lucy and I'll be looking after you two tonight. What can I get for you?'

'Can we have the bottle of the Judd's Hill Napa merlot —'

I cut in. 'Oh, remember I won't have red.'

'Does that mean I'm not allowed to order it?'

'No, I just thought you might want to get a glass instead of a bottle because I won't help you.'

'A bottle of the Napa merlot, the buffalo for a beginner and then the squab.'

'Arse-om choices,' says Lucy.

'And can I have a glass of the Selby Sundance sauvignon blanc, the blue prawns to start and the trout for main. Can I have the trout with the brussels sprouts that usually come with the chicken, instead of the risotto?' I ask.

'Of course. That the lot?'

'Yep,' says Sam.

'Arse-om. Won't be too long guys,' Lucy says. Her eyes loiter on Sam for a split second too long.

'I hate brussels sprouts,' Sam says.

'Really? They're my favourite vegetable. I like how they taste kind of dirty.'

He abruptly gets up to go to the bathroom. I accidentally start picking the black nail polish off my thumbnail and instantly regret it. No wonder I rarely get manicures — I can't be trusted. I'll have to scratch off the whole lot now.

We eat our first course pretty much in silence. I watch Sam as he continues to fill up his glass. The bottle is already two-thirds gone and he has a red-wine stain on his top lip.

'What's squab?' I ask as Sam offers me a taste of his main.

'Pigeon.'

'No way! It is not.'

'It is. Come on, try it. I promise it's better than brussels sprouts.'

'No thanks. Pigeons are pests, it would be like having a bite of a rat.'

He looks at me with a raised eyebrow and continues eating.

'Excuse me, is there a napkin around I could grab?' I ask Lucy as she walks over to check on us.

Either I didn't get one, or Sam has stolen mine.

'Um, I'll go check.' She looks as if she is about to crack up laughing as she walks off. Sam is also smiling.

'What? I don't get it. What have I missed?' I ask.

'No, nothing. So come on! Ask me things, I'm wide open.'

I feel like a journalist being granted an all-access pass to Sam's mind. Maybe then he will ask me some questions and my standby list of answers will finally see the light of day.

'If you were to get in a cab on your own, would you get in the front or back?'

'I don't catch cabs.'

'But if you were to?'

'The back.'

'Right. That says a lot about a person,' I say.

'What about you?'

'Always the front. I'm from the country. Everyone from regional Australia is chatty. Cab drivers are usually really lovely.'

'I've never met a lovely one. So what does that say about me, Sunny? That I'm an asshole?' He slurs slightly on the word. 'If you were me, you would get in the back.'

'Yeah, probably. If I get an ant in my tea, I just pick it out; I don't make a new one. What about you?'

'I don't drink tea and don't have ants at my house,'

Sam says, looking away.

Lucy reappears at the perfect moment. 'I asked the other waitress, and no, neither of us have one,' she says quietly to me.

'None at all? In the whole restaurant?'

'No, I don't think so, no.'

'Oh, that's odd. Okay, that's fine.'

'Translate into American, Sunny; she doesn't know what you mean,' Sam says loudly.

'I'm just after a napkin to wipe my hands on,' I say, pointing to Sam's.

'Oh, a serviette!' Lucy says, dashes off and comes back with one. 'Can I get you some dessert?' she asks, as she clears our plates, looking as if she is about to crack up again.

'Not for me,' says Sam.

No! Dessert is the best part! I can't be a piggy on my own.

'None for me either,' I say.

Damn.

'Just another bottle of that Napa merlot. Do you want another drink?' he asks me.

I shake my head.

'Arse-om. Thanks, guys,' says Lucy.

'What did I say that was so funny?' I ask.

'Napkin.'

'Why is that funny?'

'Here it means, you know, sanitary napkin, women's stuff.'

'Oops,' I say, laughing myself.

Sam is not laughing and his eyes are glazed.

'Hey, are you sure about another bottle of wine? This

will be your fourth, Sam.'

'You drink, too, Sunny.'

'Yeah, but that is a huge amount of alcohol. Don't you think you've probably had enough?'

'How would you know what is enough for me? You actually don't even know me,' he says and stands up.

He's right; I don't at all.

He pays the bill and takes the wine to go. He finishes the bottle in silence in the car and falls asleep. I wake him once we arrive at the condo and he looks at me as if he has never seen me before. He heads for the kitchen and I head straight up to my bedroom.

'Goodnight,' I call out to no reply.

I wake up feeling dry all over from the central heating. It is almost 11.00 a.m. but I don't want to go downstairs. I listen at my bedroom door; it seems to be silent outside. I fill the spa bath in my ensuite and have a very long soak. I see how many seconds I can hold my breath underwater, and try to pick off the rest of my nail polish.

I finally tiptoe downstairs, but there is no sign of Sam. I make a coffee and watch a bit of TV. I start getting bored and by one o'clock I wonder if he is even here. We were home and in bed before midnight last night. Could he still be sleeping?

I creep up to his room and listen at his door. Silence. I knock.

'Yeah.'

'Can I come in?' I ask.

'Yeah.'

I open the door and he is lying on his bed with his back to the door. I stand in the doorway.

'Sorry,' he says, not rolling over.

'You're okay.'

'No, I'm not.'

I walk around the bed and sit on the chair on the side he is facing.

He still doesn't look at me. 'I was sober for almost six months before last night.'

'Oh god, I had no idea.'

I get a flash memory of him trying to say no to champagne on the plane, and me insisting it was compulsory.

'I was a jerk last night, wasn't I?' he asks.

'Yeah,' I say with a smile.

He smiles back in a sad way.

'I'm so sorry.'

'Were you a big drinker?'

'Yeah. Lost years of my life to it. Lost my relationship, lost jobs, lost friends.' His head twitches. Twice. 'All that rehab, all those meetings, everything down the drain.'

'It's not the end of the world. Relapses are really normal, from what I hear.'

He closes his eyes.

'What made you drink yesterday?'

'I thought I'd be okay to just have one glass of champagne with you. What a fucking idiot! I love drinking more than anything or anyone, and I think I always will.'

'Well, that's not true. If it were, you would have drunk yourself to death by now but you didn't: you got sober.'

We go downstairs. I make him a coffee, and light the fire with the button.

'Sorry, sorry, sorry, sorry, sorry —'

'Stop. Apology accepted,' I say.

'Were you thinking: "My god, what's happening?"'

'Yeah, a bit.'

'Were you thinking: "Please god get me away from this animal?"'

'Not really, but you were a completely different person.'

He puts his head in his hands. 'It's because you're the first girl I've liked in a really long time,' he says with his head still in his hands.

'You can't say it's my fault.'

'Oh god, I didn't mean it like that, no. Shit, Sunny, that came out totally wrong.'

'How about I give you some reiki?'

'Is that like energy healing or something?'

'Yeah.'

'No, I'm not really into that sort of thing.'

'I know it sounds esoteric, but it will help. My washing machine was pronounced dead by the repair guy and I brought it back to life through reiki.'

Sam laughs.

'It's true, I promise! I just sat there with it, gave it some reiki, and it started working again.'

'What is it with you and your clotheslines and washing machines?'

He lies on the floor and I sit cross-legged at his head, putting my hands on his forehead. I have only ever done a weekend reiki course with my mum, but whenever I have tried it on anyone I've always had a good response. He lies still with his eyes closed. He has bits of sleep in his eyelashes and looks like a little boy.

I sit on an armchair in the overheated ski-hire shop and sip on a complimentary bottle of fancy sparkling water, while Sam takes forever deciding on his skis.

Finally he walks towards me with two pairs.

'Oh no, not for me. I'll just sit and watch,' I say.

'It's one of the best runs in the world. Don't you ski?'

'I've never even seen snow before. This is my first time.'

'What? Hang on, are you serious?'

'Yeah. I told you that yesterday.'

'No, you didn't.'

'I did.'

He walks away, puts my set of skis back and returns with a sleigh.

Uh-oh.

'No, Sam, I'd really prefer to watch.'

'You have to; it's compulsory,' he replies.

Shit.

We make our way to the slope, and my teeth won't stop chattering.

'Are you sure this is a two-person one?' I ask as he forces me to get into the sleigh.

He slides in, straddling me from behind on the short plank seat.

'Yeah. You ready?' he asks, putting his arms around my waist.

'No! Don't we need helmets?'

'No. You will love it, I promise.'

'No! I know I won't. I don't want to do this,' I say, trying to stand up and wiggle out of his grasp.

He holds me there. 'Why don't you want to?'

'Because I'm a scaredy cat.'

This is madness; I don't want to die here with Sam in the snow. Before I know it we are off.

Again I feel like I am freefalling,

Again I have a man behind me that isn't Tobey,
And again I don't like it at all.

Exhausted, we flop on a lounge each and watch *Entourage* on HBO, and I can't work out if I love or hate it. Out of the corner of my eye I see Sam putting tablets in his mouth.

'What was that?' I ask.

'What?' he says, taking a sip of water. He is a terrible liar. How did he make so much money from acting?

'The tablets you just put in your mouth. What were they?'

'Something to help me sleep.'

Within about ten minutes his eyes are shut. He has a concerned look on his face. I think you can tell a lot about a person's nature by seeing them sleep. One of my younger sisters always sleeps with a smile on her face.

I go and get the doona from his bed, to put over him.

'Can you come in?' he asks with his eyes shut.

'In where?'

'Here,' he says, opening his arms.

I slip in and he cuddles me from behind.

'You are one of the nicest people I have ever met,' he says into my hair, and I somehow drop into a weird half-sleep.

The next morning there are kisses being placed on the back of my neck. With my eyes still closed I roll over to face him. I slowly open my eyes and we look at each other. He has sex written all over his face. He leans in and kisses me, without me really kissing him back. He tastes like a foreign country. His hand reaches straight under my jumper and inside my bra.

I stop him.

'We can't do this. We can't have sex,' I say.

'Why not?' There is something different in his eyes.

'I just, um, can't.'

'I think you want to.'

'Even if I did want to, I still wouldn't.'

'You're not making any sense. I'm asking a really simple question: "Why don't you want to have sex?"'

'It just doesn't feel right.'

'It will be lovely, I promise you.' He starts to kiss me again, and I pull away.

'No, Sam.' I get up to leave the room.

'When you start something, then cut it off all of a sudden, I think there needs to be an explanation.' He is used to getting exactly what he wants.

'You started it, I didn't start it.' I go into my bathroom and run the shower. I have it as hot as I can stand.

What am I doing? What was I thinking coming away with someone I barely know? Of course he expects me to put out. I stay in the shower for a long time, until I look like I have given myself a full-body first-degree burn. I turn the water off and sit curled up on the cold tiles. There is a knock at the bedroom door.

'Yeah?' I call out.

'I made you a coffee.'

'Thanks.'

'I'll leave it at the door,' he yells.

I stay sitting on the tiles for another few moments, then wrap a towel around me. I open the door to see him still standing there with the coffee in his hands.

'You're really red,' he says.

'I know.'

'I was a total jerk before. I just wanted to have sex with you so badly. I was irrational. I'm sorry.'

'It's okay.'

'I have something fun organised for you, if you want to get dressed,' he says and smiles again in a sad way.

The main street, called Main Street, has a magical village-type feel. Everyone is rugged up, and there is electricity in the air like the day before Christmas. We pull into a little lodge and a perfect blonde woman comes out to greet us.

'Saaaaaaam! So good to see you! And you must be Sunny. So good to meet you. Aren't you gorgeous. Sam, she is so beautiful. I LOVE your jacket! I'm Suzannah, by the way.'

'Nice to meet you,' I say.

She is the kind of woman who brings all of my grubby bits to the surface, like the stubborn chips of black nail polish that refused to come off and my fly-away hair that I didn't get time to blow-dry.

'Come this way and we'll sort you out.'

We enter a lodge, which looks like some kind of market, and have a model each to carry our 'swag'. I'm still not quite sure what we're doing. The woman at the first stall leaps out and waves at us to get our attention.

'Would you like to try on some boots?' she asks me.

'Um, sure.'

'Which ones do you like?'

'Um, the brown ones are nice.'

'Great choice! They are *sooooooo* comfortable. They are fur-lined, and amazing to wear in the snow. You will not slip in these, I can promise you that.'

I try them. They're lovely.

'They are so cute on you!' she squeals. Suzannah and the two models all chime in. 'So cute.'

'You could have some to match,' the woman at the stand suggests to Sam. He shakes his head, but she refuses to take no for an answer. She dresses us in matching beanies, scarves, jackets and mittens.

I start to worry how much this is going to cost. Will they be giving us a discount? Will Sam offer to pay?

All of a sudden the woman starts taking our photo with a very bright flash.

'Come on, put your arm around her,' she says, picking Sam's arm up and putting it around me. She takes one of Sam with his arm around me, then he walks away looking extremely unamused.

'Okay, moving on,' Suzannah says.

I thank the woman from the stall, and she prints out one of the photos and hands it to me, which I put in my jacket pocket.

'How does this work?' I whisper to Sam. 'Do we have a tab and pay afterwards?'

'No, just grab what you want.'

'What, so it's all free?'

'Yep.'

'Are you kidding me?'

'Nup.'

I have waited my whole life for this moment: to find myself in a real-life 'gifting lounge'. Holy shit.

'We have the iPhone in pink,' the man at the Apple stand announces.

'Um, sure. Yes please,' I reply. Ah!

We move on to make-up. Sam announces he is going outside to make a phone call. I sit down to have my hair and make-up done by a man who has had plastic surgery to look like Sandra Bullock.

'I'm going to do you a huge favour, sweetheart. I promise you, you will be thanking me forever. Do you give me permission to change your life?'

'Sure.'

The next thing I know Sandra is shaving my face. I mean literally shaving with an electronic shaver. He assures me it is a special hair remover for women, which means it won't grow back spiky. He sends me off with a huge bag of products and looking like I may be a burn victim with a good three layers of heavy-duty foundation coating my face.

I go to a jewellery stand and pick out a pair of

diamond earrings, and a gold chain with a fan-shaped jade pendant. Again I have my picture taken with the product. Little do they know, as I smile down the lens, that I am a big fat nobody. This is the same rush I experienced when I shoplifted as a teenager. I feel as if I'll be discovered as a fraud at any moment and have everything taken off me, which gives me a sense of urgency.

Suzannah escorts me along to the next lodge. There's more? I pick out underwear, iPod speakers, a dressing-gown, cashmere wraps, and little handmade Guatemalan dollies. We move on to the next one. Where's Sam? He's missing out. I go from scared to scarily greedy in a very short space of time. I choose some baby clothes, even though I don't know anyone with a baby, and get annoyed with the girl at the jeans stand when she doesn't have the ones I want in my size. I pick out sheets, trainers, organic candles, bamboo towels and a bikini.

I walk out into the glaring afternoon, and as all of my 'swag' gets piled into the back of the car I start feeling dirty, as if I have just stepped out of a strip club. Oh my god, what just came over me? I have taken too much.

I call Sam, who has met up with some friends at a nearby bar and says he has put my name on the door. Leroy drives me back to the condo to drop off all of my bags and then takes me to the bar. As I am getting out of the car he passes me his card in case he can 'do anything else to make my trip more comfortable'.

The place is dark and reminds me of a cosy Melbourne wine bar. There's a large black chandelier hanging in the middle of the ceiling, and a piano being played by a man in a tuxedo next to a roaring fire. Sam is sitting in a booth in the back corner with a big group of people.

'Hi,' I say.

'Oh, hey.' Sam is sitting closest to the wall, and things look squeezed as it is, but people move along and I sit on the end. He introduces me to everyone. I recognise the tiny blonde girl sitting next to him named Charlotte. I have seen her in several films; she is the definition of a 'packet-cake actress': predictable, artificial and boring.

'How did you go?' he asks me.

'Really good, it was amazing.'

'What did you do, bella?' Charlotte asks me.

'I went swag shopping.'

'Right. Good for you,' she says in a patronising tone, as if I have just announced I am on unemployment benefits. 'I will never forget my first Sundance. I had this beautiful little film opening, and I went to my first swag lounge. I was *so* excited. I was given some free diet drink and they tried taking my photo with it. My manager literally dragged me out and wouldn't let me get anything. I got *sooooo* sad, then I got really mad with him and begged him to let me back in, but he promised I would thank him in the long run. Imagine if there were photos of me going around now, posing with a can of sugar-free soft drink!'

Everyone laughs. She has a diamanté hook on the side of the table, from which her bag hangs. This one detail alone grates on me so much I can barely look at her.

'Would anyone like a drink?' I ask in a nervous voice.

'Yeah, can you get another bottle of the Chalone pinot noir?' one of the guys says.

Sounds expensive.

'Yeah, sure.' I look up and see an almost empty glass of

red in front of Sam. He sees that I see it. I shake my head at him. *Don't*, I mouth.

'What was that?' he asks me out loud.

Brave. He must have had quite a few already. Everyone looks at me. He's so lucky I am a nice person.

I go to the bar and order the wine, and a juice for me. The drinks are also free. I place the bottle of red in the middle of the table. Sam's glass is the first to be filled.

Everyone has now moved on to some story about a director that I have never heard of. I try to strike up a conversation with the guy next to me.

'Sorry, I just have to hear the rest of this story,' he cuts me off.

The story ends, and he doesn't come back to me.

The afternoon continues on. Sam manages to avoid eye contact, and not one person makes an attempt to include me in the conversation. It's like I'm completely invisible.

Everyone stands. Apparently the opening of a French film is about to start at the Egyptian Theatre.

'Don't do this,' I say quietly to Sam.

'What?'

'Drink, Sam,' I say a bit louder. 'You don't need to do this. Let's just get out of here. I'll get some stuff and make us some dinner back at the house.'

'I'm not hungry and I want to see this film,' he says, looking straight through me.

'Do you want me to come, or would you just prefer to go with these guys?'

'Up to you.'

I traipse along to the Egyptian Theatre, which apparently was the first sound-movie cinema in Utah.

Again I am seated on the end, six seats away from Sam, who is again seated next to Charlotte. The film is slow and hard to follow. I let my eyes have a little rest.

I hear applause and snap awake. The director and actors make their way up the front for a question-and-answer session with a translator. I wipe the drool off my chin, with the sleeve of my jacket. American after American raises their hand to put in their two cents on the film. I think they speak to hear the sounds of their own voices, rather than to actually ask a question.

We all make our way to a club for a private party. I am disoriented, wonky and overtired. I escape to the toilet, and find myself washing my hands in a basin next to Charlotte.

'What did you think of the film?' she asks.

'I actually fell asleep.'

'Are you serious? It's like the film of the year! It's a masterpiece. The director is literally a genius. How did you sleep through it? Are you one of those people that doesn't like foreign films?'

'Well, I am a foreigner so, no, I'm not "one of those people".'

'Right. Do you want some coke?'

I can't think of anything worse.

We sit down together at one of the little antique tables with a mirrored top in the powder room. I agree to snort up a chemical storm in an attempt to wake up some sort of personality. No one blinks an eyelid at us. She has line after line. I stop at two and head back out to the party. My mind and the room slow down, and my body and heart speed up. I walk straight up to Sam. He is mid-conversation. I wait, then get bored of waiting.

'Sorry to interrupt, but can I talk to you for a minute?'
I ask.

'Sure. This is Alex. Alex, Sunny.' He introduces me to
the guy he is with.

'Nice to meet you,' I say and Alex smiles.

'What can I do for you?' Sam asks. He has another
red-wine stain on his upper lip.

'Can we talk over there, just for a sec?'

'About what? Don't you need to ask Alex if he has a
clothesline?'

'No.'

'Come on, Sunny. Ask him, he won't bite.'

'I don't want to.'

'What do you want to talk about then? Alex knows a
lot about me, so you may as well say what you need to say
right here.'

'I think you should stop drinking.' Alex cracks up
laughing. 'Is that funny, is it?' I ask him.

'Yeah, it is. Who is this chick?' Alex asks Sam.

'Sam's an alcoholic. Did you know that about him?'

'Aren't we all!' Alex replies, then clinks Sam's glass.
'Cheers.' He gives him a high five.

'Anything else?' Sam asks.

'Are you ignoring me because you know I'll try and
stop you drinking, or because I didn't have sex with you
this morning?'

'I'm not ignoring you.'

'Oh, come on.'

'How am I supposed to know how much attention
you need and when you need it?' Sam says.

If I'd had sex with him would it have confirmed that
we have chemistry? Would he make sure I was cast in the

pilot? Would it launch my career in America and give me enough money to set me up for life?

I head back to the toilet because I have no one else to talk to and nowhere else to go. On my way there I get a sudden, sharp pain in the upper part of my stomach. It catches my breath. Could it be menstrual pain? No, wrong time and wrong spot. My whole body tenses in panic. I try to deepen my breath, but uh-oh it's getting worse.

The pain doesn't let me stand upright; I am slouched over struggling for sips of air as I walk. I get into a cubicle and sit on the toilet with my head in my hands. It feels dangerous and not like anything I have ever felt before. Is it from the cocaine? How could I have been so stupid?

Oh holy shit, it's getting worse and worse, and I can't see properly through my watery eyes. What on earth am I going to do? I'm stuck in the snow in the middle of nowhere, and I don't really know anyone. Oh no, I definitely need some sort of help. I need to get myself out of this cubicle and back to Sam. No, I can't. I'm too embarrassed and he won't want to help me. He'll think I've made it up, as an excuse to interrupt him again. I close my eyes and force myself to take deeper breaths, which help a tiny bit.

I get myself up and out of the cubicle. I still can't stand up straight because of the pain. I scour the room for Sam, and can't see him anywhere. He couldn't have left without me, could he? I circle the room for a second time, then see a doorway with a rope across it and a bouncer guarding it.

'Sorry, ma'am, this is a private section,' he says.

'Do you mind if I just go in for a second? I'm looking for someone.'

'I can't let you in, I'm sorry.'

'Please? Just for thirty seconds. I promise I'll come back.'

'Still no, ma'am. I'm going to have to ask you to step away from the rope.'

'Here, I'll leave my handbag with you and if I don't come back within thirty seconds you can keep it. There's quite a bit of money in there.' My eyes start watering; the pain is getting worse.

'This is the United States of America, ma'am, and I have no idea what's in that handbag.'

'Oh my god, I swear there's no bomb in my bag. Look, you can check for yourself,' I say, opening my bag. 'I'm actually not very well and I have to find my friend.'

I look past him and see Sam towards the back of the room, sitting with Charlotte. 'Sam!' I yell out. He looks up and catches my eye and looks away. 'See, there he is, that's my friend Sam. I know him,' I say to the bouncer.

'So do a lot of young women,' he says.

'Sam!' I yell out again. He doesn't respond, so I decide to phone him. I watch as he takes his phone out of his pocket, looks at it and rejects the call.

'I'm going to have to ask you to leave the premises,' the bouncer says.

'Are you serious?'

'You can leave of your own accord or be escorted out.'

'It's okay, you don't have to force me. I'll go.' I burst into tears as I walk out into the snow. People stare at me, and no one offers to help. I head up the street looking for a taxi but can't see any, and also realise I didn't even write down the address of where we're staying.

I sit down on a park bench and try Sam's phone again, which is now switched off. I get colder and colder.

Suddenly I remember I have Leroy's card in my bag. I call him and within a couple of long minutes he is pulled up in front of me.

'What happened?' he asks, as I hop in the front.

'I'm not very well. Can you take me to a doctor?'

There are no doctors' offices open at this time of night so he heads for a hospital.

18

We drive for about half an hour before pulling up outside a fancy building. It has two levels and the reception area looks like a hotel lobby.

'I need to see a doctor really quickly,' I say to the woman at the front desk.

'Do you have insurance, ma'am?'

Oh no. When I bought my ticket I decided to take the gamble and come away without it.

'No, none.'

'Okay. You'll need to fill out this form.'

'Can I do that afterwards? I'm really sick. I think something bad has happened.'

'Absolutely not, ma'am. I need you to fill this out before you can see a doctor.'

I sit on a chair doubled over and recite my details to Leroy, who fills out the form for me.

'I will need to get a credit card from you, to hold on to while you are being treated,' says the receptionist.

'Can I just ask how much this is going to cost?' My hands start to shake as I get my card out of my wallet. I only have about a thousand dollars left in my account.

'I can't tell you that, I'm sorry.'

Will they stop my treatment when they realise how little money I have on that card? Should I call my mum?

'I need to know,' I say in a surprisingly deep voice.

'We take a partial upfront fee for seeing a doctor, then you will be billed for the balance, depending on what you have done.'

'How much is the upfront fee?'

'Four hundred dollars.'

Leroy waits in the foyer and I am led into a room with four other beds in it. A voluptuous black nurse draws the curtain and gives me a robe to put on. A female doctor comes in and asks me standard questions, which I am familiar with from the medical crash course I took for the hospital show that George and I were in. I consider keeping it quiet but decide I have to confess to having used cocaine. She presses various points in my stomach — and one point in particular in my upper abdomen makes me scream.

Just when I think the pain can't get any worse, it does. I have now surpassed the point of physically being able to cry and even talking hurts too much. The only thing I can do is tap my ring on the metal bar on the side of my bed.

'What would you rate the pain out of ten?' the doctor asks.

'More than ten,' I immediately reply. 'Can I please have some painkillers?'

'I'm sorry, I can't give you anything until we have a better understanding of your condition.'

'I feel like I'm dying.' Tears drip from my eyes. 'Am I going to be okay?'

'You're going to be fine,' she tells me and strokes my hair.

They do a blood test and a urine test. While we wait for the results I concentrate on the ceiling.

'What are you thinking about?' the nurse asks.

'I'm counting. Backwards,' I whisper.

'How come?'

'Instead of having no idea what's coming next, when you count, at least you know what number is coming next.' I am still whispering.

My tests, when they return, apparently show nothing.

'I need something for this pain, please. I can't live through one more minute of it — seriously.'

The doctor gives me some tablets to take, which I immediately throw up. She gives me another two different ones, which I also throw up. Then a doctor from upstairs comes down to give me an injection.

'This is Jeff. He is the only doctor allowed to administer this drug,' the nurse says.

'This drug' does the trick. I can feel the warm liquid fill up my body, like a peaceful white lake.

My grip on the bed's metal bars loosens, my hands float down beside me and my eyes fall shut.

'Are you okay?' I hear a voice from somewhere ask. I smile. Everything solid from beneath me melts away and I am cocooned. My pain is instantly thawed out. I understand why people become addicted to pursuing this state; it is pure sailing happiness.

'Sunday? Are you feeling any better?' the nurse asks.

I slowly feel myself coming back up to the surface. I open my eyes, wondering how long they have been shut.

'Yeah, the pain has completely gone.' I'm a lot calmer and am seeing everything through different eyes.

'That's good news. Now, because they haven't yet

found the cause, the next step is to do an MRI.'

'That sounds expensive. I don't have any insurance. Do you know how much it will cost?'

'I don't. Accounts can tell you that information.'

'Can you get someone from accounts to come and talk to me?'

The nurse returns and tells me there is no one from accounts working at the moment; they start back at 6.00 a.m.

I ask her approximately how much it will cost, and she says for legal reasons she isn't allowed to quote me a figure. I tell her I have no money and do not come from a wealthy family, and she tells me there are financial plans I can go on to help 'people like me'. I ask her if she thinks I will be okay to leave without getting the MRI done and she says she wouldn't recommend it, but that the decision is obviously up to me.

I suddenly remember poor Leroy and find my phone and call him. He is still waiting in the foyer. I thank him but tell him to go and that I will call him when I'm ready. I call my mum, who instantly panics. She says she is going to get on a plane.

'No, no, Mum. I'm okay now. I just need advice on what to do.'

'Do every test they think you need, darling, I will pay whatever it costs. Your health is the most important thing at this point.'

'Okay.'

'Why don't you get on a flight straight back here?' she suggests.

I ask the doctor, who says I shouldn't fly until we have a better idea of what's going on.

I decide to go ahead with the MRI. We have to wait for the on-call specialist to arrive, who has the machine on a truck. Hours go by where I cannot eat or drink. I'm starving, but the pain is still non-existent. The specialist arrives and wheels me out through the snow on a thin metal bed and up onto his truck.

I recognise the MRI machine from the movies. As I am moved through a big revolving metal circle, there is no triumphant music playing; I wait for the moment where I'm struck with a grand realisation of my life's purpose, but it doesn't come.

Finally I am taken back to my bed. The specialist who has to look at the scan is in New York, and we have to wait to hear back from him.

My phone rings; it's a private number.

'Hello?'

'It's me.' Tobey sounds quiet.

A tear runs down my cheek. I can't speak.

'Your mum called me. What's happening now?'

I go through the whole story (minus Sam and the cocaine) and I can tell he is worried. He tells me to get whatever tests I need and offers to give me his credit card number.

'I just want to say how sorry I am, Tobey. I'm sorry I was indecisive. I can't imagine how horrible it would have been for you. I am so sorry I broke our little family.'

'It's the worst thing I've ever been through.'

'Do you hate me?'

'No.' There is a long silence.

'Hey, remember how I used to make you do a dance to the sound of the blender when I made my morning smoothie?'

He laughs. His laugh is like drinking hot melted chocolate while on a diet.

'When I come back ... Can I come home?' I ask. Silence. I hold my breath.

'Let's not talk about this right now. You rest. Call me when you find out what's going on.'

Apparently the MRI results don't show anything out of the ordinary. They do an ultrasound where nothing unusual shows up either. No one can give me even the faintest idea what's wrong, and I am still feeling better, so I make the decision to leave.

I get Leroy to stop off at a petrol station on the way back to the condo, where I buy two boxes of honey-flavoured graham crackers.

At the condo I open the door quietly, but there is no sign of Sam. I put a blanket around myself, watch the sun rise over the snowfields and polish off the crackers with a glass of milk.

I leave no note, and use up the last of my money on a flight back to LA and excess-luggage fees. As the plane takes off I feel my cheek. Sandra Bullock lied: it did grow back spiky.

Growing up, we went to a restaurant about once a year. Mum would bring a large bottle of Just Juice orange juice in an esky in the boot of our Volvo, and all four of us girls were forced to stand around the boot and have a 'big drink' from the bottle, because we weren't allowed to order a drink once we got into the restaurant. Buying drinks at restaurants and someone meeting you at the arrival gate inside the airport are two things I still find special. Mum isn't stingy but she is also firmly against paying for parking at airports.

As I walk through the arrival gate at LAX Nina is there waiting for me, even though I insisted against it.

'I've got so many presents for you,' I say as I lift the second box off the baggage carousel.

Nina drives me north of Hollywood, towards the Valley, to a public hospital. They charge a flat fee of one hundred dollars and see anyone.

'We have to make sure you're okay. I'm not calling your mum to tell her I've found you in your bed, face down and blue,' Nina says.

'But I'm fine now, seriously,' I say.

'Well, you won't be when we walk in the door of the

hospital. The sicker you are, the quicker they see you. This is going to really test your acting skills.'

'No, I'm not going to lie to the doctors.'

'Yes, you are. People wait there for over sixty hours.'

We arrive after about an hour and a half.

'Pretend you can't walk and start crying,' Nina says and puts her arm around me as if to hold me up.

I have crocodile tears streaming down my face and am taken into a small room for an initial assessment.

'We need to see a doctor immediately,' says Nina.

'So does everyone here,' the nurse says, tonelessly.

'I feel like there is something seriously wrong,' I put in.

'You deserve a Logie,' Nina whispers to me as the nurse writes her notes.

We are sent out into the waiting room. Nina's sixty-hour estimate wasn't an exaggeration; most people look like they have been here for days. White is not the dominant skin colour, and there are bossy signs on the walls. The room is full, bright, loud and smelly. There are bleeding people, crying people, homeless people and sleeping people. It's like being in a mixed-sex prison cell in a third-world country.

One man is trying to ask for something from the woman at reception, who is behind glass. He's yelling and banging on the glass, and she is carrying on with her work, ignoring him. There are no seats left, and half the people are sitting or lying on the floor.

We find a little space against the wall next to a Mexican family. The linoleum is cold, and the little boy's computer game next to us is very loud and very repetitive. Nina and I don't speak much.

Hours float by. Nina goes off on little trips and manages to locate the one guy in the room who is semi-good-looking. He's French and she flirts with him even though he's just had a motorbike accident and torn open his shoulder. She finds a kiosk, which doesn't sell magazines but does sell lots of 'candy'.

We borrow a pack of cards from the family next to us, play a game called Spit, and eat too many peanut-butter-flavoured lollies. A doctor appears from behind the magic blue swinging doors every hour or so. Each time the doors swing open the doctor is assaulted with harassment and pleas from the waiting patients. We pause our card game and look up and pray the words 'Sunday' and 'Triggs' will be called out.

'Oh crumbs,' I say, losing yet another card game.

'Crumbs? Who says crumbs?' Nina asks.

'Me.'

'I've never heard you say that before.'

'I got it from Tobey. He doesn't use it properly though, like when he trips or spills something; he only uses it when something goes really wrong, like when someone he knows has had a heart attack.'

'I can't believe you used to let him win at cards.'

'No, I didn't,' I say.

'You did. Remember that camping trip to the Blue Mountains? We played Canasta and Tobey was sitting to your left and you kept throwing out cards that you knew he needed.'

'Did I?'

In the toilet, *I LOVE JESUS* is written on the back

of the door in thick black pen. Would Jesus be opposed to graffiti? Any publicity is good publicity, right? My leg muscles shake as I make sure I don't touch the actual seat. The toilet looks as if it hasn't been cleaned in quite a while, and touching it would guarantee an instant urinary tract infection.

Nina has a sleep. I stay on the lookout in case my name is called or in case someone attempts to roll us. Somehow a fire catches alight in my mind. How? There are no matches or lighter in sight. It starts off small and seems manageable but within seconds the wildfire is engulfing everything in sight. *My life is not looking how I thought it would look.* Every decision I make is wrong and pulls me backwards yet again. I left school too early and have no skills, no degree, no savings, and now I'm single. If the world went to war, what good would I be? I am a pointless person; a Post-it note that doesn't stick. Why did I choose this profession? I can't change careers now and go to university with eighteen-year-olds. My life is arranged solely around trying to get acting jobs — all for what? I may never get another job, and I'm not actually skinny or good-looking enough to be an actor.

After fourteen hours my number comes up. We walk through the magic doors and it's like walking through the gates of heaven. My Mexican-American female doctor, who looks younger than us, is lovely and seems to be genuinely on my side. I tell her my story about the previous hospital and she thinks it's appalling that they didn't tell me how much the treatments would cost. She examines me, does a blood and urine test, and I give her the MRI results to look at.

'Thank you. My god, what would I do without you?

You are such a good friend,' I say to Nina as the doctor goes off to write up a report. Tears come into my eyes again. She comes and lies next to me in my bed and gives me a long hug.

'People are going to think we're lezzos,' I say.

'Good,' she says and we both fall asleep.

'What did they tell you in regards to your MRI results?' my doctor asks as she returns. I wake up with a drool trail down the side of my mouth and into my hair.

'They told me that nothing unusual was found,' I say.

'Well, these results are overexposed and impossible to read, so I'm not sure why they told you that.'

She goes on to say that the blood and urine tests are both normal, and that there could have been a small twist in my bowel, which would explain the sudden onset of pain. Due to the fact that my pain has now subsided she thinks I'm okay to leave.

Nina puts the one-hundred-dollar fee on her credit card, and we are sent on our merry way.

'Don't you dare tell anyone about my twisty bowel. How embarrassing.'

'What are you doing up?' I ask Albert as I walk in the door.

'I couldn't sleep. Can I make you a cup of tea?'

'Yes,' I reply and flop down on the couch.

He makes a pot of peppermint tea and brings out a plate of choc-chip cookies. I take him through the entire story, from Sam's drinking to the trips to the hospitals.

'Why didn't you call me?' Albert asks.

'Um, I didn't want to bother you.'

'Bother me? That's what I'm here for. Did the hospitals try and bill you on the spot?'

'I paid an upfront fee at the first hospital, and they are going to bill me for the balance.'

'And how are you going for money, if you don't mind me asking?'

'Not very well.'

'Well, at least let me help you in that department.'

'No, no, Albert. Thanks anyway.' I dip another cookie into my tea.

I finally make it into my own bed and grab an extra doona to put on, even though it isn't a chilly night. My head is thumping, as if I've spent too long in a nightclub. I reach up for my phone as it chimes with a new voice message.

'Hi baby, just wanting to see if you're okay. Have been talking to your mum and she said you're a lot better … Um, yeah, speak to you later.'

It's Tobey, and his voice sounds the same as when we were together. I replay it over and over before falling asleep.

I wake up and call Tobey, even though I know it's the middle of the night in Australia. It goes through to voicemail, and I leave a short, slightly tense-sounding message. I look out the window and onto my first stormy day in LA.

I decide to jump in the car for a drive, to witness everyone's long faces, but the weather has made everyone even happier. People in Starbucks are beaming and loudly commenting on the 'arse-om' weather. Can't anything rain on their parade? I guess antidepressants are pretty strong.

I prefer stormy to sunny weather, even though my name is Sunny. I love it when it's so stormy you have to turn the lights on in the morning. I grew up in the country and if I woke up to the sound of rain it usually meant a day off school. We lived in a high-flood area and often got rained in.

I walk along with my grande chai latte in hand, which is so sweet it makes one eye go squinty every time I sip it. I stop outside a wedding-dress boutique and stare at one particular dress through the window.

Before I know it, the shop assistant is zipping it up my back and I am staring at myself in it. I look hard into my eyes and wonder if this is possible. What sort of wife would I make? Am I ready for the back door to be bolted shut? I can't be a person with a failed marriage. I want a marriage where you throw out undies well before the elastic goes, and where boobs and bums don't go saggy. Is that what millions of women before me have also wanted? Will I slip straight into that 'married' category and wake one morning to find I've stopped bleaching my moustache, reassuring myself it was never that bad, and decide my laser hair removal is too expensive? Will Tobey still love me if I am a bit chubby with a mo'?

I wonder if there is a particular point you hit where you're absolutely sure you've met the right person, but even if there is, how can you promise that you will feel like that forever?

When Mum got married there wasn't a flicker of doubt in her nineteen-year-old mind, and she still says that she never regretted marrying my father. She was brought up by her nana Poppy, who had meals on wheels delivered to her by my dad. For the first few weeks the only words exchanged by my parents were my dad saying 'meals on wheels', and Mum nervously snatching the tray and saying 'thanks'.

One day the doorbell rang and Mum (who always got a bit dressed up for when he came) answered the door and he wasn't there. She saw him sitting in the back of his truck with the roller door up. She walked towards him and saw that he had a little rug spread out in the back with two meals-on-wheels meals set out (with their plastic lids on) and a candle in between them. They were married shortly after.

I walk back towards my car and put my hands in my

jacket pockets, where I find the photograph of Sam and me at the gifting lounge. We are in matching wintry outfits: Sam has his arm around me and it looks like we could be on our honeymoon in the snow. It is a really sweet photo, besides the fact that Sam looks like he is about to murder someone. Just as I go to put it back in my pocket I pass a rubbish bin and decide to slip it in there instead.

On my way home I pop into the 7-Eleven to buy a phone recharge card.

'Where are you from?' asks the man behind the counter.

'Australia. Have you ever been?' I ask, knowing the answer. I read somewhere that only ten per cent of Americans have travelled outside their country. They are the richest and least-travelled of the developed nations. I wonder if it's because they don't have to travel far within their own country to experience different cultures; or maybe we've all come to them, so they don't need to come to us.

'No, I have never been to Australia. So have you guys, like, got your own pop stars?'

'Yeah. We even have our own *Australian Idol*.'

'That is so neat!' He laughs and laughs.

Wow, I should do stand-up. I hand over my Visa, only to find it is rejected. I have never gotten used to having an empty bank account, although I probably should have by now. It is such a hollow feeling, like I don't have the right to be alive. How do I still let this happen at my age? What is wrong with me? I should never have come overseas.

I get home, and after checking my emails, I do some

research on the internet and find I could fetch around fifty thousand dollars to sell my story. *Sam falls off the wagon over me*. Again, he is so lucky I am such a nice person.

'Stayed at a hotel with Two-day-Ray last night. He's phasing me out, I can tell,' Nina says, sitting on my bed clipping her toenails onto a magazine.

'Good.'

'He's had me thinking he's been away on tour, but last night I caught him out; he's been in LA all along.'

'What can I say, Neens? Good.'

My phone rings. It is an extremely cheery, young American man informing me I can get fifteen per cent off my medical bill if I pay it today with a credit card over the phone. He also informs me the balance owing is twenty-two thousand and three hundred dollars. I stop breathing. I inform him that my hospital visit in Salt Lake City was a complete waste of time and that they couldn't tell me what was wrong with me. He says the hospital has passed the bill on to the collection agency he works for and that he can't discuss my treatments.

'Sunny, someone's up shit creek without a paddle,' Nina says as she clips her little toe and I see the nail go flying.

'I'm not up shit creek; I'm not paying the bill. No way.'

'Sell your story,' Nina says. I've given her a blow-by-blow account of Sam and his drinking at Sundance. 'Fifty grand is fifty grand, it's a no-brainer. Then you can pay the bill!'

'No, I can't do that to him.'

'What? Look at what he did to you! You could have died. How about I sell it for you? I'll say it was me, and you can give me a cut.'

'Still no. I feel sorry for him.'

We put on *Jagged Little Pill* by Alanis Morissette as loud as it will go on my computer, and get dressed up to go to a party for Australian expats in LA. Both of us still remember every word on the album, and sing along loudly and out of tune but filled with passion.

We walk through a busy jazz bar, up a narrow staircase and into a function room filled with Australians. There is so much ambition and desperation in the air you can almost feel it on your skin.

'So good to see you!' Shelly appears in front of me, looking even shakier than she did when I had a coffee with her at Fox Studios.

'How are you?' I ask.

'I'm amazing!' she says with an unconvincing smile. 'I have been going for meetings with agents this week and they've all gone so well!'

'You know what they say: never a bad meeting in LA.'

'I am *so* in love with LA.'

'What do you love about it?'

'Well, the people, for a start. Don't you love how encouraging everyone is?'

'People shower you with compliments in this city

because they want you to compliment them back,' I say as I see George out of the corner of my eye. He sees me, and my breath catches in my chest. We both instantly look away.

'What about In-N-Out Burger, don't you love that place?' Shelly asks.

'It's just the same as Hungry Jack's, which I never ate at home, so why would I eat it just because I'm here?'

What is it with positivity that evokes this reaction in me? Why do I instantly turn into a sad sack?

'I've got a DVD for you to watch. It'd be really good for where you're at, right now. It's called *The Secret*.'

'No thanks.'

'It's phenomenal. You can have anything you want. Your thought patterns actually create your own reality. If you're stuck in a negative thought pattern, that's what will come to you in your life: negativity.'

'So, say if a girl gets raped, she's responsible for that? She brought it on herself through her own thought patterns?'

'Um, I'm not sure about that …'

'I'm going to go and get another drink. Are you right for one?' I ask.

'I'm fine, thanks.'

I make my way to the bar. Gosh, I know that was a bit rude but I just couldn't stand to be in that conversation a moment longer.

'Excuse me.' A youngish Australian guy touches my shoulder. 'I wanted to say I thought you were incredible in that film about the girl that loses her mum. But you probably already know that,' he says with an embarrassed laugh.

'Thank you.'

As an actor I don't think you ever really know — acting is so subjective. No matter how many compliments you receive, it's never enough. It's the bad reviews that stay with you, like a neon sign that flashes on and off. A sign that flashes so brightly that you can see it through your eyelids when you are sleeping.

I order a glass of tap water from the bar, partly because I haven't been able to drink since being at Sundance with Sam, but also because I can't afford a drink. It's good to be in a room filled with familiar faces for a change. I go from one fluffy conversation to the next, which all start out sugar-coated, but have one very clear agenda: to extract information. Who is your management? Do you have an agent and a manager? Have you had any call backs or work yet? Overnight success is a lot more possible here and there is a clear divide between the few Australians who have actually got work out here and flourished, and the rest of us who are madly treading water.

A guy named Guy comes up and gives me a big hug. He graduated from a good drama school in Australia but only got one offer from a small agency. He hung around for years in Australia selling wine over the phone, pretty much unable to get an acting job, but within months of coming to America, he was signed on to a big television series about vampires. We used to call him the Jack Russell, because he used to be like a little Jack Russell humping your leg every time you saw him. I did like him but always found myself shooing him away.

'Wow, look at all these Australian actors wearing black. You go to Americans' parties, and there is colour everywhere,' I say as George appears next to Guy.

'Give me black any day over some of the crazy shit the Americans wear,' George says, giving me a kiss on the cheek. 'How are you, mate?' George asks shaking Guy's hand.

'Yeah, good. Bloody flat out but good,' Guy says.

'I love the way Americans wear whatever they feel like, without caring what people think,' I say.

'You wear what you want without caring what anyone thinks,' George says.

'No, George, I don't.'

'What do you hold yourself back on? Bear heads?'

'No, tap shoes. I want to wear them all the time: to the movies, to the shops, everywhere, and I always think about them,' I say, and George smiles.

Even though I wasn't very good, tap dancing was my favourite thing growing up. Mum would never let me wear my taps outside the dance hall; I wasn't even allowed to practise at home, in case I damaged our floors or my taps.

'Anyway great to see you both,' Guy says and moves off.

The air changes.

'So you're alive, that's good news,' I say.

'Yeah, why?'

'Just thought it was a bit weird that I never heard back from you.'

'When did you call me? I don't think I got a message.' Something flickers, ever so slightly, in his eyes.

'Even if you didn't get a message, wouldn't you have thought to call me?' I ask in a raw voice.

'I've been a bit busy.'

'Right.' I'm an idiot. George has girls around him

all the time. Of course he wanted to have sex with me; he wants to have sex with every girl. It doesn't make me special.

'I hadn't seen you in almost a year and we had a good catch-up. Sorry, I didn't realise I was expected to call you.'

'No, that's fine.' I smile as hard as I can. 'I'm just going to go to the bathroom.'

I sit on the toilet seat staring at the wall in front of me. Was that reasonable to ask why I hadn't heard from him? Or did I come across as a creepy obsessive desperado? I think maybe the latter. Maybe I've created a whole story around him that doesn't actually involve him. Did I just completely freak him out? I carried on as if we'd slept together! All we did was kiss, and it was practising for an audition scene, so it doesn't even count.

Uh-oh, I have totally embarrassed myself. Why did I get all serious on him? Was I trying to create drama for the sake of it? I should just wrap heaps of toilet paper around my head and tiptoe out of the party.

I find Nina to tell her I'm leaving (having not gone with the toilet-paper idea) and unfortunately she's not ready to go. I get out the door and see George standing in a group having a cigarette. I smile and he smiles back. I walk to my car on my own and look back to see if he is coming up behind me. No. I am not living in a romantic comedy. Keep walking. Why am I in this heartbreaking business? How much longer can I sustain it? As long as you are acting, the treadmill is switched on. You have to keep running because if you stop, even for a second, you are pulled backwards and thrown off.

I peel my sweat-drenched Bikram yoga clothes off and reach for my phone at the same time. One missed call from my manager. I listen to the message; the television pilot didn't go our way. I call her back but she is 'unfortunately away from her desk'.

I get home and find an envelope filled with fifty-dollar notes on the doorstep of my outhouse. The thought of accepting money from Albert makes me sick, but I literally didn't even have a dollar for the parking meter at my Bikram class today. I'll just borrow a little bit, and pay him back when I can.

I make a strong coffee, go out and buy a recharge card for my phone, and then spend hours ringing around trying to find someone to discuss my medical bill. I hate doing boring things. Especially boring tricky things. Finally, after several different wild goose chases, I find out there is a hospital close by that is actually a sister hospital to the one I went to in Salt Lake City. No one at the hospital will discuss my bill over the phone, so I'll have to go in person.

On the way I decide I should stop by my car-hire place and swap the PT Cruiser for something cheaper.

I spend quite a while wandering around looking at the various hire cars.

As an actor I always feel like I am permanently in a state of being up for hire. Will I still be hired out if I'm married? Will it somehow affect my value? I actually couldn't give a shit anymore. I am so sick of basing all my decisions around trying to get acting work and trying to get people to like me.

I stop by the cheapest car I can find. It's a white bomb that looks like it could have a body in the boot. I wave to a Mexican man with no teeth who comes over, and I tell him I will take it.

At the hospital I am told that there isn't anyone who can discuss my bill.

'What about you?' I ask the lady behind the glass.

'I have no authority to access your file.'

'What about someone from the accounts department?'

'We don't have an accounts department here, ma'am.'

'There has to be something I can do?'

'Good luck, ma'am,' she says, closing the glass window and walking away.

I sit in the waiting room. I'm not sure what I am waiting for. There are big pink comfy couches to sit on and a bunch of pink carnations in one corner, which are my least favourite flower as they remind me of death. There is nice cool air-conditioning and no one is bleeding or crying.

I go to the vending machine and get an instant coffee, which has built-in sweetener. I fiddle around with my iPhone, bite off all my nails and finally decide to leave.

I walk outside and see a man with doctor-type tags around his neck. He is talking on his phone so I wait patiently right beside him.

'Hang on,' he says into his phone. 'Can I help you?' He is about forty, and kind of handsome.

'I hope so but I'll wait.'

He goes back to his conversation and I wait. And wait.

'What's up?' he says, when he has finally finished on the phone.

I explain my story. He plants me back in the waiting room and goes off to see what he can do.

About half an hour later I am led into an office and introduced to a woman named Bev, who has big hair, big shoulder pads and big nails. She has my file out in front of her and there is something maternal about the way she listens to my story.

'Okay. There are a couple of options. First one is to pay the fee upfront, and you will receive a substantial discount. Second one is to apply for a payment plan, but seeing as you are not an American citizen or disabled I highly doubt you will be eligible.'

'What about if I just skip the country? I don't care if I'm never allowed back into America,' I say.

'We are linked to debt-collection agencies all over the world. You wouldn't ever be able to get a cell phone in your name back in Austria or a bank loan —'

'Australia. I'm from Australia. I can't pay this money. Can't you do something about the bill? They couldn't even tell me what was wrong. Hospitals are free in my country. I had no idea it would be this much.'

'I wish I could help you but I don't have the power to change your bill. Once the hospital has passed the bill on to the collection agency it's non-negotiable.'

'Oh my god.' I burst into tears. Bev passes me a box of

tissues. Did I really think this bill was going to evaporate into thin air? 'What if I get a lawyer? And take this to court?'

'My dear, unfortunately the cost of your legal fees wouldn't make it worthwhile.'

'Michael Moore didn't cover this in *Sicko*. I was talked into getting treatments, and refused information on the price. I've been completely ripped off.' I effortlessly cry and cry. I blow an accidental snot bubble and have to turn away because I start to giggle.

We go back and forth, me pleading with Bev, and her giving me sympathy but repeating over and over that she can't help me.

'Let me go and make some calls,' Bev says and stands up.

'At Salt Lake City they told me the MRI results came back as normal, but the doctor at the next hospital told me the MRI was overexposed and impossible to read,' I say as she is walking out of the room.

The magic last-minute words. Who would have thought that this one detail alone could clear my debt completely?

Bev has a doctor look at my MRI, who also deems it unreadable. With the discrepancy between this fact and what it states on my report, my bill and my case quickly starts to crumble. I am asked to pay a two-hundred-dollar fee and Bev says we'll be all square. I can't get my envelope of fifty-dollar notes out quick enough.

I get outside and mouth *thank you* to the sky. That was my highest-paying performance yet. Twenty-two thousand, one hundred dollars' worth of tears.

I am woken the next morning by a loud croaking noise, right near my ear. It takes me a few moments to realise it is the new ringtone on my iPhone.

'Hello.'

'Spelt?'

It's Tobey. Spelt became his nickname for me after our first date, when I dragged him along to a health-food café and ordered a spelt sandwich.

'How are you?'

'Good, Tobe, just waking up. Are you out? It sounds loud.'

'Yeah. What's your answer?' He is drunk.

My god, it is good to hear his voice.

'You are,' I say straight away.

'Yeah, that's your answer now, but as soon as you get another acting job I lose you again.' He is very drunk.

'No, you won't.'

'How do I know for sure?'

'You just have to trust me.'

'I don't know if I can trust you. I don't think I can do this anymore, Sun. I think we have to let this go.'

'No! No!' I sit up and am suddenly very awake. 'What

are you doing? Don't do this — you are all I care about.'

'I can't keep hoping. I can't do it anymore; it's killing me.'

'You called to ask me what my answer is and I told you that *you* are my answer. Now you're saying no? I will get on the next plane home.'

'Don't. Even if you do come back, I don't think I could ever feel like you were mine. We have to have trust, and I don't think I can trust you.'

'Of course you can!'

'I asked you to be my wife and you didn't say yes. I'd been collecting those white stones for so long …'

I can hear a quaver in his voice.

'I love you, okay?' I say and bite my lip as hard as I can. 'Whatever happens in my life, my mind always comes back to you.'

'I've gotta go,' he says.

'Don't go, please. It's me. Listen, it's just me.'

'I do have to go, bye.' And he hangs up.

I stare at nothing for a long time, then get into a bath that burns my skin. I've had what I've always wanted all along. Maybe part of the problem is that I've taken it for granted, because up until now I've never had to fight for it.

How long does it take to get bedsores? I hope I get one; at least then I would have something to show for my five days in bed. The last time I tried to leave the house my car got towed for being parked too close to a fire hydrant. They didn't move it to a legal space a few blocks away, like in Australia; they impounded it on the other side of the city. They offered a discounted rate if I was able to get there within the hour. How? You can't catch public transport because you might get stabbed, and taxis don't really exist. I have banned myself from the outdoors. I can't cope with another thing going wrong.

I watch an ant crawling up into my water glass on my bedside table. I reach over and squash it. I feel no guilt. I could never be a Buddhist. I can't be a Christian or an atheist either. I don't even know what I believe in.

When we were young my great-aunt took us to Sunday school, and after she died I tried picking up Christianity again. I started going to church on my own every Sunday, and praying every evening. I loved the sense of community and purpose, but after one particular service, which gently spelt out that gay people wouldn't go to heaven, I walked out and never went back.

I have told Albert everything. He's had a front seat, watching me chain-smoke in my pyjamas for almost a week, and hasn't once told me to pull my socks up. He's taught me how to play chess — and we've played games that go on for days. I've worked my way through every film Albert has ever written (which were all pretty terrible) with my two new best friends: peanut-butter-cookie-dough-flavoured Ben & Jerry's ice cream, and Cinnabons.

Albert quietly assured me that this storm would pass. I quietly disagreed with him. I always thought Tobey was the one constant in my life, but he's not answering my calls or emails and my heart is physically hurting. (That may also have something to do with the number of cigarettes I am smoking.)

Every time I try to call Maryn, her assistant says

she is away from her desk, which translates as I've been dumped. It's the worst kind of break-up: a deathly silent phase-out without the decency to actually tell me. Seeing as I never got an offer from an American agent, my one connection to acting here has now been severed. I can't help but think she may have received some bad feedback from the chemistry test. What was I thinking with that wee story?

I know I need to get out of here, but the thought of setting up on my own in Sydney makes me sick. Maybe I should just move back in with Mum in Bellingen; she could teach me how to bake bread and I could live a really simple life working at the bakery.

Albert bans me from the house for the whole afternoon. When I am allowed back in he blindfolds me and I am led into the lounge room, where I can hear loud Mexican music.

'And open!' he says, untying the tea towel from around my head. The room has been decorated in a brightly coloured Mexican theme with a donkey piñata hanging near the window next to an inflatable cactus. Albert wears a sombrero and has maracas in his hand.

'Happy birthday!' Nina jumps out from behind the couch.

'You two! You shouldn't have gone to all this trouble. I didn't want to do anything for my birthday this year!'

Nina hands me an envelope. Inside the card there is a plane ticket to Mexico.

'Free next Thursday?' she asks.

'Ahhhhh! This is too much, Nina!' I give her a hug. 'I've always wanted to go. I can't believe it!'

Albert hands me an envelope containing a voucher for Fred Segal, which is embarrassingly generous.

We sit down to chicken mole and very strong lime margaritas. I can't stop smiling and thanking them both.

After dinner the lights go out, Nina brings out a birthday cake with candles, and the three of us sing. On the cake, written in icing, it reads: *Happy Birthday then underneath Sunny*.

'I don't get it,' I say, after I blow out the candles. I have no idea what to wish for.

'When I ordered it over the phone from the little Filipino baker, I said, "I want the words 'Happy Birthday', then underneath, 'Sunny', written on the cake." He took it literally. I didn't have the heart to ask him to fix it up,' Nina explains.

Nina teaches Albert and me the macarena. Then, while we unsuccessfully attempt to smash open the piñata, the doorbell rings. Albert goes and we continue to beat the poor little donkey with a wooden spoon.

'Sunny!' Albert calls.

I go to the front door and see George standing there with a box in his hands.

'Happy birthday,' he says handing me the box.

'How did you know it's my birthday?'

'Facebook.'

I take the lid off the plain white box and undo the pink tissue paper to reveal two black tap shoes. I feel like I am about to cry but manage to swallow it. Why is everyone being so nice to me? I don't deserve any of this.

'Oh my god. Thank you!' I say, hugging him.

We go inside. Albert makes George a margarita and insists he has a bowl of the chicken mole.

'How did you know my size?' I ask George, as I try them on. They are a perfect fit.

'Asked Nina on Facebook.'

George is the one who finally smashes open the

piñata. Old, weird-looking fluorescent lollies pour out and I make everyone have one. We ditch the Mexican music, and I go up and get my iPod to plug in through the speakers. The four of us dance. I'm amazed at how versatile the macarena is — it fits in with 'Low' by Flo Rida and 'The Doorbell' by The White Stripes. Albert still has his sombrero on and uses his maracas to accentuate his moves. Nina takes over as DJ and the real hits come out from The Veronicas, Beyoncé and Britney Spears.

Albert announces he is ready for bed, so Nina, George and I go up to my outhouse. I check my phone: still no birthday message from Tobey. I go through cigarette after cigarette in an effort to smoke out and kill that niggling thought.

George pulls out a joint, which the three of us share. Even from just a couple of drags I get quite stoned. It could have gone either way: I could have gotten stupidly paranoid, but luckily it calms me.

'Jeez, this is one expensive guitar,' George says, picking up a guitar in the corner of the room.

'Albert is one rich man,' Nina says.

'Can I have a go?' he asks.

'Yeah, if it works. I'm sure Albert won't mind,' I say, sitting down sideways on the big cane armchair with my legs dangling over one side. 'Can you play my favourite one?'

George does a version of Joni Mitchell's 'A Case of You', which usually guarantees him any woman in the room. He always seems to whip it out towards the end of parties and you see women's minds ticking over and imagining what their baby with him would look like. He goes on to play 'Throw Your Arms around Me' by

Hunters & Collectors, 'Fake Plastic Trees' by Radiohead, and 'Round Here' by Counting Crows and we sing along.

On my computer Nina looks through the proof sheet of my latest headshots. The photographer is apparently the best in LA and charged thirteen hundred dollars for a two-hour session. He asked me to bring along the most revealing clothing I owned and insisted I drink a glass of champagne on arrival. He advised me, in all seriousness, to 'make love to the camera'.

'Have these been touched up?' George asks.

'Look at my real face, George,' I say, and the three of us crack up laughing for no reason. 'Honestly, how old do I look?'

'Early to mid-twenties.'

'Now look at the photos: how old do I look?'

'Twelve.'

'There you go, you answered your own question. I didn't even ask him to touch them up. I can barely recognise myself. He got rid of my freckles and everything. I look like one of those everyday boring overly made-up teenagers. He should have given me some big boosies while he was at it.'

We are all on a one-second delay from the pot. My god it feels good to be out of my head.

'I've got a dare for you, Sunny, and once you do it you can dare me to do anything,' George says.

'Why is everything a bargain or a competition with you?'

'Like what else?'

'Wearing that bear head was part of a deal, not to mention the "tally board".'

'What's the tally board?' Nina asks.

'When we were doing the medical show, he made up a chart with all the main cast's names on it and every time someone stumbled or forgot a line, he would jump up and run to the green room to put a mark next to that person's name.'

'What? In between takes?' Nina says.

'Yeah, when we were in the studio and we'd all have to wait for him. The person at the end of the week with the most strokes had to buy a slab.'

'Miss straighty-one-eighty here only ever got one stroke,' George says.

'Which didn't even count because I'd just been to the dentist, and had a numb mouth.'

'You still stumbled on your line; rules are rules,' George says. 'Okay, come on, your dare. You have to agree to it before I tell you what it is.'

'I do. Agree,' I say a bit too quickly.

'You have to put this headshot up on Facebook as your new profile picture, and update your status to say: *Sunday Triggs is wondering what everyone thinks of her new headshot that she has just had done in Hollywood!* And there has to be an exclamation mark after Hollywood.'

'NOOOOO, no, George, I won't do that, anything but that. I can't do that, it goes against everything I am. I've never even filled in that "update your status" section. *Please*, no, don't make me.'

George and Nina force me to and watch me do it. I will lose every drop of street cred in one fell swoop. Nina starts throwing dares back at George. Each suggestion involves something filthy, which I shut down. Nina suddenly remembers she has her personal training session early the next morning, and George decides to leave also.

I walk them out. Nina gets into her car first and George lingers.

'Do you remember me telling you about the short film I wrote?' he asks.

'Yeah.'

'Well, the private funding came through last week and I'd love you to read it. I kind of wrote it with you in mind for the female part.'

'Yeah, sure, email it to me. I'd love to read it. Have you cast the male part yet?'

'Yeah, me.'

He drives off and I keep waving until his car is all the way out of sight. Was waving for so long like that a normal thing to do? Or am I really stoned?

Did George come over last night only because he wants me to do his film? I open the attachment on his email and read the script. It's called *Hunter* and is about a woman named Zoë, her son Hunter, and his father Ryan. Zoë lives in a small town and falls pregnant from a one-night stand with Ryan, who is passing through. Zoë calls Ryan to tell him that she is planning to have the child, but at that point Ryan says he doesn't want anything to do with the situation.

Five years on, Zoë and Hunter now live in Los Angeles, due to the incredible success of her jewellery line. Ryan now decides he wants to be a part of Hunter's life and comes over to spend some time in LA. After an introduction period, Ryan starts having Hunter to stay some weekends. Zoë sees a change in her son for the better.

After Ryan has been in LA for some time, he invites Zoë out to dinner, just the two of them. They have an undeniable connection. He drives her to Santa Monica Beach where they go for a late-night swim, kiss in the waves and then he stays the night at her place.

The last scene of the film is Zoë and Hunter having

breakfast together, while Ryan is in the shower. Hunter asks his mum if she went through any cat flaps for his dad. Zoë asks him what he means and he goes on to explain that on the weekends when he stays with his dad, they go to different people's houses when they aren't home, and his dad sends him to crawl through cat flaps. He lets his dad in the front door and goes and waits in the truck. He says his dad helps people who have been locked out of their houses.

'It's good, George,' I tell him on the phone.

'Thanks. I think it will be about a twenty-minute film and it's obviously non-union … Um, what else do you need to know? The budget's not huge, but we can pay you, illegally. It will be a five-day shoot starting Monday week. Are you free?'

'Yeah, I think I am.'

'Do you want to do it?'

'Yeah, okay.'

'Cool. We confirmed the little guy playing Hunter the other day; he's perfect. I want to do a read-through this Wednesday afternoon. Can you make that?'

'Yep.'

'Great. Oh, and on Wednesday night after the reading I have a friend's potluck birthday party, if you want to come?'

'What's potluck?'

'Everyone has to bring a plate of food.'

'Um, maybe. I'll see how I go.'

I flick over to Facebook. There are seven new comments from people about my new profile: *Wow, you look great!* and *Good luck in La-La Land* etc. Whenever someone says 'La-La Land' my opinion of them drops.

Plummets, actually. I just can't bear it.

Oh dear, everyone thinks I'm serious: they think I've been lost to the world of positivity junkies. I better go home soon to set the record straight. I quickly change my picture back to my original one, where I'm pretending to have a lazy eye.

I hold my breath and open up my online banking page. Just as I am about to exhale, I stop: I see a nine-thousand-and-forty-three-dollar credit from my agency back in Australia. I click over to my email account and find an unread message from one of my agents, congratulating me. A car ad I did last year has rolled over. Oh, thank you god. I can pay Albert back.

'Thanks again for these,' I say to George as he answers his front door.

'They look great on you,' he says, looking down at my new black shiny taps.

'I brought this plate for the potluck,' I say.

'Devilled eggs? What are you, a seventy-year-old?'

'People love them; they're my speciality.'

'If they don't all get eaten by the end of the night, you have to eat the whole lot yourself. Deal?'

'What are you? A seven-year-old?'

We do a read-through of the script. Luca, the young boy who plays Hunter, is great. The script reads well, and it's a real relief to be acting in an Australian accent again.

Later we go up a few flights of stairs and enter a dimly lit bohemian paradise smelling like nag champa incense, with tea-light candles everywhere. I imagine these are the kind of little parties Joni Mitchell sang about in LA in the 1970s.

'Aussie George!' A girl leaps up and hugs George for quite a long time. Still hugging.

'This is my friend Sunny. Sunny, this is Paige,' he says once the hug has ended.

'Hi, nice to meet you. Thanks for having me,' I say, as she hugs me also.

'You're Aussie, too! Oh my god this is sooooo sweet! You two are so beautiful! I'm so happy to have you both here for my birthday!' Her face is lit up like the sun and there is bliss vaporising from her pores — she looks like she is on very good terms with this world.

'Happy birthday!' I say and hand her the plate of devilled eggs.

George passes her a bag of Pirate's Booty, a kind of Cheezel-type snack.

We are given plates, which we pile up. There is a feast of dahl, brown rice, tofu, tempeh, curry, soup, dips, falafels and colourful salads.

I sit on a little daybed with George, and we have our plates on our laps and mugs of punch on the floor. I scan his plate: no devilled eggs. I give him one of mine.

'You may be having a few more than that,' he says, referring to my eggs. 'You better get spruiking.'

'Excuse me,' I say to a guy sitting near us, who has hair down to his waist. 'You should try some of the devilled eggs; they're really yummy.'

Long-haired men are as bad as big-bummed men.

'I'm vegan.'

'Oh. What about you then?' I ask the girl sitting next to him, who also has hair down to her waist.

'I'm vegan, too,' she says with a sympathetic smile.

'Oh. Is everyone here vegan?'

'Yeah, pretty much.' she replies and turns away from us.

Poor old devilled eggs.

'Did you know the birthday girl is a vegan?' I ask George.

'Nup.'

'How do you know her?'

'Just from around.'

'Have you rooted her?'

'No,' he says, looking offended.

I thought he would think that was funny.

The birthday cake is an organic, wheat-free, sugar-free, vegan red velvet cake. It is dark pink, coloured naturally with beetroot. It tastes like shit.

'Okay, now it's time for the best part,' says the long-haired vegan girl. 'I hope you've all got your artistic gestures prepared for Paige! Who would like to start?'

A guy with skin-tight, high-waisted green jeans and a perfect blonde quiff puts up his hand and everyone cheers.

'Did you know about this?' I whisper to George.

'Yeah, I forgot to tell you. You are meant to have prepared an artistic gesture, instead of bringing a birthday present.'

Shit. Surely I won't be expected to get up and do something.

Two chairs are placed facing each other on the sectioned-off imaginary stage. George hands me another mug of punch and we go and join everyone else sitting in a semi-circle on the floor.

The guy with the quiff gets Paige to sit in one chair, and he sits in the other. They sit there silently staring into each other's eyes for about a minute, until a single tear rolls down his right cheek. He wipes the tear off his face and into Paige's hand.

'Happy birthday, Paige,' he says, standing up. He hugs her and she lifts her feet off the ground and wraps them around his waist. Everyone claps and cheers. Paige has tears in her eyes. She gives him a long kiss on the lips.

'Okay, this is for Paige for her birthday but also for Pocket, my dog that had to be put down last week,' says the next girl who gets up.

She has set up a chair and a table with a mug on it. Instrumental Indian-sounding music starts. She stays very still, just looking at the cup, then in a swift movement she goes to pick up the cup and stops right before she touches it and jerkily turns away from it. She starts to do some sort of quick birdlike head movement in time with the music, then drops to the floor dead still for quite a while. Everyone's eyes are transfixed on her. All of a sudden up she leaps and starts doing a sexual motion on the corner of the table.

Out of the corner of my eye I see something moving: it's George's shoulder shaking. He is slightly in front of me so I can't see his face properly. I lean forward and see he is laughing, the silent forbidden kind; his face looks strained, as if he is trying to hold back diarrhoea. He sees me and the strained look gets even worse.

It is infectious. I bite my lip and stare at my lap and try to think of something sad. It doesn't work. My shoulders are now shaking also and I start to sweat. There is nothing funny about this feeling; it's painful and horrible.

Finally the interpretive dance ends, and the clapping and cheering gives us some sort of relief. There are only twelve of us here, which makes it impossible for us to slip away unnoticed.

'Together let's create the soundtrack to Paige's life,' says the next girl up.

We are all instructed to sit in a circle, join hands and close our eyes. We are to harmonise organically with each other to create a symphony. Thank god George isn't next to me.

It starts off with some low humming, which I join in with. This is good. I am under control; I just have to focus. Things start building and all of a sudden a girl's voice breaks out really loudly with: 'Oh birthday girl, you are the light that guides us, you are the living expression of pure peace.' She has the worst voice I have ever heard.

I get the laughter wave back again and open my eyes to see George looking at me. Everyone else has their eyes shut. Just for a moment we look at each other and everything stops. I have never met anyone else who shares my sense of humour like he does.

He starts laughing again and I have to close my eyes. The giggling takes hold of me, too, and this song seems to be never-ending. Tears drip down my face, but I can't wipe them away because I am holding hands with the people either side of me.

'Are you okay?' the guy next to me asks, when it finally ends.

I know I have mascara running down my cheeks.

'Yeah, it's all just so beautiful,' I reply, and he gives me a hug.

I excuse myself and go to the bathroom and wash my face. We have to get out of here.

'Time for the Aussies to get up!' Paige says when I walk back into the room.

Uh-oh. Please no.

George jumps up and does a Maori wedding dance, which involves lots of tricky clapping and slapping. I have seen it many times. It is very impressive and gets a great reception.

I can barely look at him because I am so worried about having to get up. My palms are sweating and I can feel my face going red.

'Sunny's turn!' Paige says.

Everyone looks at me. I can feel myself semi-leaving my body.

'Oh sorry, I didn't know we had to do something and I haven't prepared anything,' I say in a shaky voice.

Please, let's get out of here.

'You have to!' Paige says.

'I can't, I can't do anything.'

'Yes you can! Yes you can! Yes you can!' They all start to join in on the chant.

I can't breathe properly. I look at George: he isn't chanting but he isn't jumping to my rescue either.

Paige grabs my hand and drags me onto the stage and leaves me there. It is silent. Everyone is staring at me and I feel like I'm drowning. I stand there staring at my feet. I can't do anything. I am a nothing person, I don't have anything to offer.

Actors are meant to be able to deal with these situations. George is going to think I am such a freak. I try desperately to think of something to do, but it's like my mind has a stutter. I close my eyes and try to take deep breaths, which helps.

I begin to tap one of my feet. With my head down I start a tap-dance routine that I somehow manage to remember from a dance concert when I was young. It ends and everyone screams and cheers and jumps on me.

'Can we please go now?' I whisper to George.

'Yep,' he replies.

We say our goodbyes and I have to take my devilled eggs with me, because they are on one of Albert's good plates.

'Do you want to come on a recce for the film?' George asks once we are in the car.

'Now?'

'Yeah.'

'Um, sure.'

We drive on freeway after freeway till we arrive at Santa Monica Beach. We strip off to our underwear, then run and jump into the freezing water, the same way Zoë and Ryan do in the film. I dive straight under, which gives me an instant ice-cream headache.

'I'm too shy to be an actor,' I say.

'That's the beautiful thing about you. You're not up yourself like all the other actresses are; you don't give a shit.'

'Well, I obviously do give a shit because I have hair extensions.'

I go under a wave and swim out towards the horizon. I feel something latch onto my leg and I scream underwater at the top of my lungs. I swim up to the surface and see George right behind me.

'You are such a prick!' I say.

'I'm sorry,' he says and hugs me.

I try to struggle away from him. His arms are strong. We look at each other, then he lets me go. People always look their best with wet hair I think.

'You're a strong swimmer,' George says.

'I think it's important. I've always thought I am going to make sure my daughter is a strong swimmer, too.'

'I've always thought I am going to make sure my son is a strong swimmer as well. Maybe they'll be brother and sister,' he says.

I laugh. We both start to freeze, so we make our way out.

'Strewth!' George yells out as chilly air hits us.

'Did you just say "strewth"?' George nods. 'You just went up a notch. I love that word,' I say and he smiles.

'Hey, seeing as we probably won't have time for rehearsals on the day, should we have a quick one now?' George asks.

'Rehearse what?'

'This is the point where Zoë and Ryan kiss as they are getting out of the water.'

'No, George.'

'Come on, just a quick one. We'll do it in character so it doesn't count.'

'I don't trust you not to slip in the tongue,' I say. 'The only way I'll do it is through my hand.' I put my hand up, and in our sopping wet underwear on Santa Monica beach at midnight, George pashes the back of my hand and I pash my own palm.

The Mexican air is like a hairdryer on number five pointed right at our faces. Nina and I find ourselves a bungalow on the beach in Puerto Escondido, with two matching, faded-purple hammocks on the deck and two strict single beds. The utensils in the little kitchen haven't been washed up properly, and there are bugs, ants and flying things everywhere.

My guidebook says this is one of Mexico's best beaches. The sand is too hot to walk on and is made up predominantly of shells; the water is a dark green; there is a rip; and the waves are big and crash hard onto the shore. It is a relief to see some fat rolls on the beach as opposed to the starving, plastic bodies of LA. Our token swim is very quick, then we find some free sun beds at a café on the sand. We order coconuts to drink and swap phones to look through each other's text messages. We do this every now and then in order to dig out some dirt that either of us has forgotten to mention.

'What's this one from Two-day-Ray? *Look under the mat*?' I ask.

'There were keys under my mat and a Prius out the front,' Nina says, not looking at me.

'Why?'

'He bought me a new car.'

'What? What's wrong with your car?'

'Nothing. I just always wanted a Prius.'

'Why didn't you tell me?'

'It only happened the other day. I haven't told anyone — I feel like a prostitute.'

'Why did he buy it for you?'

'It was a parting gift, his wife's pregnant. At least I know it's definitely over now.'

'Shit! Can I delete his number then?'

'Um, I will later. What's this one from George? *I want to stand with you on a mountain, I want to bathe with you in the sea, I want to lay like this forever, until the sky falls down on me.* Sent at 1.49 in the morning, Sunny!'

'Oh no, it's not exciting at all. We were trying to remember the name of a song George sang to me once at karaoke. They're the lyrics to 'Truly Madly Deeply' by Savage Garden. We were out the other night and he texted me just after he'd dropped me home.'

'Do you fancy him?'

'Nup. We're quite similar. It would be like being in a relationship with myself. No thanks.'

'But you get on so well.'

'Yeah, well, I get on with lots of people. It's like he has this direct channel to pure genius, but then all of a sudden he realises it and gets in the way of it. His ego kicks in, which completely spoils what I love about him.'

'Have you heard from Sam?' Nina asks.

'Nup, not a peep. I don't expect to either.'

'Why not? He obviously liked you.'

'He liked being able to see his life through my eyes.

Once I stopped being excited by his life, and started to see that it was actually quite tragic, he no longer had a use for me.'

'That, and the fact that you refused to fuck him.'

Our skin starts to burn so we head back to our bungalow for an arvo nap, with the ceiling fans on full bore. The less I do in my life, the more tired I seem to be.

We wake up and there's a big grey lizard in the corner of our room. The texture of its skin, the way it moves its head and its beady little eyes make me want to gag. Nina stands on her bed screaming and forces me to chase it out with the broom.

We walk into the balmy night and wander down the main restaurant strip, past street stalls and buskers and people still in swimmers who aren't on the beach. No one blinks, besides us, as an opened-back truck drives past filled with men in uniforms who have machine guns on their shoulders. I reach for my camera but chicken out.

We decide on a restaurant on the sand, and order Coronas and the seafood platter, which comes with corn tortillas, beans and rice.

'Are you going to sell your blue car?' I ask.

'Yep, and the Prius.'

'Why both?'

'Because I'm coming back to Sydney with you.'

'Are you serious?'

'Deadly. I've even given my notice at Thongs.'

'Ahhhhh!' I leap across the table and give her a huge hug. 'That is the best thing I have heard all year. Oh my god, your mum is going to be so happy.'

'Tell me about it. I told her on the phone the other night and she literally wailed. Should we get a place together? Or are you planning on moving back in with Tobey?'

'I haven't talked to him since that last phone call when he was drunk. He won't answer my calls.'

'He's just doing that to try and get some power back.'

'Nup, I think he's really pulled the pin this time.'

'I strongly doubt it. I've never seen love like yours and Tobey's. You looked after each other as if you were an elderly couple.'

I smile at her. 'What do you do with leftover love?' I ask. 'It's like having studied medicine for six years, then someone telling you that you aren't actually allowed to practise it. Does all that knowledge just get thrown in the bin? Are you expected to forget it all? I have six years' worth of knowledge on Tobey and I have no idea where to put it.'

'I don't think you should go there yet. Wait and see what happens when you actually get back. When should we leave?'

'How about as soon as I finish the film? In a couple of weeks?'

'Okay.'

The next morning we stumble across a handwritten sign in coloured pencil that reads: *Massage and iridology*. We pay upfront for the 'full package', which includes a foot wash, a one-hour massage, and an iridology session. A young girl with a hose in her hand and a blank look on her face stands in front of us. As if watering a garden, she moves the hose from my feet to Nina's feet and back again, occasionally losing concentration and wetting my skirt.

We are led into a room, with two single mattresses on the floor, which looks like someone's bedroom. I spot a stain on Nina's mattress right near her leg — sucked in. The massage is basically light stroking, and my masseuse just giggles when I ask her to go a little harder. Our masseuses chat loudly, and there seems to be some sort of dogfight going on outside.

Next I walk through a kitchen and into a little area that has been sectioned off with an orange sarong. I sit on a stool beside a stove and an older Mexican lady studies my eyes. She pulls up my eyelids a bit too hard and lets out a series of knowing 'aah's.

'You need embrace love.' Her eyes are still and honest.

I thank her, then go and sit on the beach and wait for Nina.

The waves are even angrier today. Anyone attempting a paddle is being spat out back onto the shore.

Embrace what love? Embrace whose love?

Nina finds me and we decide to walk all the way along the beach to the far point.

'I don't know how to embrace love,' Nina says.

'What? Where did that come from?'

'The iridologist said I need to embrace love, and she's right. Maybe that's been my problem all the way along: I've never really allowed love in.'

'She said the exact same thing to me! It's probably the only English she knows.'

'What? Are you serious?'

We both crack up laughing and walk on in silence. When we reach the point, we spread out our towels and spend the rest of the day reading our books. We wander back along the beach in the dark, even though my guidebook advises against it.

In bed that night I can't sleep. The sheet feels scratchy and the air is hot and still. Questions zoom into my mind like paper planes being thrown at my head from all different directions: why do I religiously drink wheatgrass shots even though they taste like falling over on the lawn? Why do I act if I'm a shy person? I have dedicated my life to chasing made-up stories, the majority of which are badly written. Maybe I just look for any excuse to run away from myself. I wonder if it's my mind and its natural disasters that I am actually trying to escape from.

The next morning we venture away from the beach and into the shopping district. We pass a church full of people dancing and singing at the top of their lungs. Men wear suits and play guitars and the women wear bright, full-circle skirts.

Our taxi drops us outside a market that goes on as far as the eye can see. Each stall is packed in underneath its own individual tarpaulin, but even the shade doesn't dull the bursting colour of the produce. I buy a painting of a Mexican wedding, which is so colourful it's like staring into the sun. You almost have to squint when you look at it.

We stop for lunch at a tortilleria. There are three large glass containers of different-coloured drinks out the front and behind a loud machine that is fed dough and churns out perfect round tortillas onto a conveyor belt. The tortillas are placed on tall piles that almost touch the roof. Women line up to buy a stack and place them straight on top of their heads.

We wait for a table — and seeing as there are only four it takes a while. There is no menu; they only serve the one dish, fish tortillas, which costs the equivalent of one American dollar. We both agree it is one incredible meal and order another plate between us.

'How's the eating going?' I ask Nina.

'Good at the moment. I'm having seconds.'

'What are the triggers, when things get bad?'

'Well, it's a disease, and I don't really know what the triggers are. Sometimes I think I am doing okay, then I'll wake up one morning and not eat breakfast and then try not to eat for the entire day, because I feel like I don't deserve to. On those days it's like if I were to put something into my mouth it would drag me even further away from getting an acting job or getting a proper boyfriend. I tell myself the less I eat the more successful I will be.'

'When you don't eat and your eyes are all glazy, you are not a successful human being, you are not a successful friend and you definitely couldn't be a successful actress.'

'I know that.'

'You are beautiful at any weight; you're looking really good at the moment.'

'Yeah, but I'll never be skinny enough. I could be on my deathbed from starvation and still think I could lose just a bit more from my upper arms, and thighs. Remember when I came back to Australia after I'd only been in LA a few months and I was so skinny that everyone called me "Skeletor" behind my back?'

'I never did, but yeah.'

'It didn't scare me or make me think there might be something wrong. I was actually thrilled when I found that out.'

'Nina! You were never this bad when you were living in Australia; it's bloody LA that's done it to you. I really want to help you get better. It's possible — people recover from eating disorders all the time.'

'Well, what did scare me was an article I read recently about an anorexic that couldn't have children because of how badly she abused her body. One of the reasons for going back to Sydney is to get some proper help.'

It's our last afternoon, and I take off on my own for a swim. Again the ocean looks angry. I go out past the waves and imagine I am being chased. The faster I swim, the faster my heart beats, which makes me feel alive. A wave comes out of nowhere and dumps me quite hard. The sea wins.

I get out, inspecting my grazed elbow and shrugging my sore shoulder. As I dry my hair with my towel my hair extension starts to come out. The one long weft has detached itself from the metal beads that kept it in place near my scalp, but because my hair is a bit matted at the back it is still semi-attached. I close my eyes really tightly and rip it out, which absolutely kills. I sit on the beach with a wet, revolting, knotty pile of peroxide-blonde hair in my lap. How did my life come to this? I have drifted so far away from the person I actually want to be.

'I want it as close to my natural colour as you can get it,' I say to the hairdresser back in Beverly Hills.

'Mousy brown? Sweetie, I flat out refuse to dye your hair that colour.' He wears high heels, tights and an off-the-shoulder top that exposes an extremely large muscle.

'Should I go somewhere else then?'

'This colour is fantastic on you. Why don't you want to stay blonde?'

'Because it's not real.'

'Honey, not one thing on me is real,' he says, as if it's something to be proud of, then goes and resentfully begins mixing up the colour.

I start on a stack of magazines. Why is it that seeing perfect woman after perfect woman makes you lose the will to live?

Finally I hand over the voucher I received in the freebie bag from Sam's premiere and emerge a mousy brunette.

As I walk to the car, I catch a glimpse of my reflection in a shop window and smile to myself. At last, a step in the right direction.

I stare at an email that has just popped into my inbox, entitled *Rosie and Mark's spontaneous barefoot Byron Wedding*. They are the couple who introduced Tobey and me. Rosie is an actress who I have known for years, and Tobey and Mark went to school together. Most of our photos are of the four of us. I have to be at their wedding, which sure is spontaneous; it's not next Saturday but the following one. They have been engaged and talking about getting married for so long, I can't believe they're actually doing it.

I change my original flight to get on one that arrives in Sydney in the early morning of the wedding day. I call Nina with the flight number and she screams loudly at the actuality of leaving America, but agrees to book a seat for herself on the same flight. Then I arrange a domestic flight from Sydney to Ballina. Yikes, I bet Tobey will be the best man.

I spend the rest of the day learning my lines for George's film, which starts shooting tomorrow. I rewrite quite a few of my character's lines, and when I read them out to George on the phone he agrees to the changes. He also admits that I am better than him.

'How on earth did you get the funding for this, George?' I ask as we are getting our make-up done. Judging by the film trucks, this doesn't look low-budget.

'I'm a sweet-talker, Sunny. Look into my sparkly eyes: that's how. And of course I fucked the right people.'

'That doesn't surprise me,' I say in all seriousness.

I haven't yet met an American that understands sarcasm, and my orange-tinged make-up artist is no exception. She looks mortally offended, but with all her botox it's hard to tell. At first glance she resembles a teenager, but her neck is the dead giveaway. She should wear a skivvy or get her neck done, too. But then she would have to get her boobs done to match if she hasn't already, then her stomach, then her bum; it's never-ending.

'Hey, thanks for telling me about your change of hair colour,' George says.

'Oh shit, I forgot. Want to fire me?'

'I would if there was time to find someone else. It does mean you're scratched off my list: I only root blondes.'

'Spewing.'

My make-up artist lets out a small cough and momentarily turns away from me.

I sit on the steps of the make-up truck, smoke a rollie and watch the sun rise. A film set is one of my favourite places. I love every detail: the busyness, the puffy jackets, the early mornings, the nerves, the catering and the new instant friends. Seeing as the Australian system is modelled on the American system, there is only one real difference that I've noticed: craft service. In the same way that I'd heard about gifting lounges, I had to see the craft-service station with my own eyes to actually believe it. It is basically a free 7-Eleven store on the back of a truck that satisfies any craving, from quesadillas to Jolly Ranchers. Australia's equivalent is known as the tea-and-coffee cart, where you can usually find a large plastic tub filled with Arnott's family assorted biscuits or, on a good day, there may even be assorted creams.

I am introduced to the director, Dirk, who is about mid-thirties and wears a pair of black Nike Air Max and a black hoodie. George was planning to direct this himself but last week he freaked out and decided to get Dirk on board.

My character's house is brand new, with floor-to-ceiling windows and a lap pool. There is not one drop of atmosphere — it reminds me of a display home. George and I do a line run, sitting on one of the perfect beige couches, then get up and do a rehearsal. I know exactly how George works: he jokes up to the very last moment, then as soon as 'action' is called it's as if this magic switch flicks.

'Action!' Dirk calls out in his huge American accent.

I have the first line and love the juxtaposition between

the booming American accent and the lazy Australian one.

We do the scene where Ryan arrives at Zoë's house for the first time. I open the front door and George hugs me, which he didn't do in the rehearsal. He goes in to kiss me on the cheek, I pull away and it is fantastically awkward. There is nothing artificial in George's eyes, and the conviction in every word that comes out of his mouth is almost disturbing; no word is given away cheaply. Each thought is visible and lands with balletic precision.

'Cut!' Dirk calls mid-take, and says he can't understand us. We go for another take, and try our best to articulate, but Dirk comes back with the same response.

George starts to stress so we take a quick break, and the two of us go to craft service for a percolated coffee, which tastes like watery dirt.

'Don't worry. No one in this country can understand our accent. I repeat myself all day,' I say.

'But I want to enter the film in festivals here, so we need to be understood.'

'We both have quite neutral accents, George. Maybe it's just him or maybe you'll have to put subtitles on it,' I say as Dirk comes up behind me.

'Guys, you're doing an amazing job, but how about trying to strip back the accent?'

Apparently this is Dirk's first go at drama. His background is in music videos and commercials.

'Mate, if we strip back our accent, there ain't going to be an American one underneath,' George says with a smile on his face.

'Look, we're not in the outback now guys. We're in Los Angeles.'

'Thanks for that piece of information, Dirk, but have you read the script? The characters are Australian,' George says, still smiling.

'Yeah, I've read the script and it is awesome. Well done, George. The problem I am having is that my two lead characters are incomprehensible.'

We stumble through the rest of the day. Despite the tension between George and Dirk, I think George will be really happy with the day's rushes. We head back to craft service and stuff down freshly baked chocolate brownies.

'Thanks for your work today,' Dirk says. 'You guys are really great together. How about the both of you have a good think about the accent overnight, and I look forward to seeing you tomorrow.'

'I don't know if there is going to be a tomorrow for you, mate,' George says.

'Excuse me?' His spotless enthusiasm suddenly vanishes.

'Come on, this isn't working. Thanks for your help today, but —'

'It is not my fault that this isn't working.'

Ouch. Hello, silver spoon.

I excuse myself and hear Dirk's voice getting louder and higher in pitch as I walk away.

Day two, the scenes are shuffled around so we do all of the Zoë and Hunter scenes, and George directs. Luca sits and watches as I get my make-up done and asks me why I don't have any real kids. I tell him I will have my own soon, and he asks when and I just say soon.

We do a rehearsal in the kitchen. Just before the take, George asks me to move a little to my left, then a little to my right, then a smidge back to my left. He goes to ask me to move again and I look up, turn so Luca can't see me, and give George the finger.

'Still haven't learnt?' George asks, referring to my glimpses down at the freckle on my right hand.

I mouth *fuck you*, and he calls action.

'Dip your finger in the mixture, Luca,' George calls out, while we are in the middle of a take.

Luca dips his whole hand in the chocolate cake mixture. I try to get him into trouble, but he quickly wipes it on my apron. I flick the spoon at him, which unintentionally goes all over him, and with George's encouragement we end up with the brown cake mixture all over the perfect white kitchen.

Luca is one of those rare children who are meant to

act. He easily acts me under the table.

After this scene Luca says he likes me more than his real mum and insists I carry him everywhere. While we are waiting for the next scene he sits on my lap and I pretend to steal his nose. I look up and see George watching us. As soon as I catch his eye he looks away.

Luca's real mum is also an actress and was on a long-running soap in Australia. They relocated here a year ago, when her director husband started to get work in American television. She asks me how much longer I am planning to be here. When I tell her that this place is all a bit much for me and that I am leaving next week, she looks quietly satisfied.

As the afternoon progresses Luca's attention span starts to dwindle, but with some extra sugar, and endless enthusiastic commentary from George on the sidelines, we manage to make it through the ambitiously scheduled day.

The next day they shoot all of the Ryan and Hunter scenes, so I'm not required. I get a text from George to say that he's got a new director on for the next three days: Katrina, who was a regular director on the medical show we were in and is in town for the month for some meetings.

That night, Albert and I go out for an early dinner. The restaurant he has chosen is in a charismatic old bungalow in Los Feliz. It is surrounded by terraces and garden patios and filled with people. I order the chopped salad with ranch dressing and Albert has the house burger.

'Didn't you ask for no onions, Albert?' I say, as he

carefully picks them off with his fork.

'Yes, but not to worry.'

My god I love this man.

'I have a bomb to drop,' I say, holding my breath. 'I've been putting off telling you. I've booked my ticket back home.'

'Oh.' He looks down and starts fumbling with his napkin. 'When do you leave?'

'End of next week.'

'Oh dear, that's soon.' He looks up and smiles at me.

'I know, I'm sorry. You have been the best thing about this trip. I wouldn't have lasted two weeks if it weren't for you.'

'Of course you would have. You're a strong little thing.' He concentrates back on his napkin and his smile fades.

'Oh no, please don't be upset. You'll finally get some peace and quiet! I'm sure it will be a relief when I leave.'

'I don't know about that, Sunny.'

Don't you dare water, eyes.

I lean over and give him a hug. I smell the sandalwood on him, which I remember smelling the first day I met him.

I go up to the counter and order the Oreo layer cake for us to share for dessert. As I walk back to our table, the word 'India' on a flyer on the noticeboard catches my eye. The picture is of a woman with curly white hair and the heading reads: *Freedom from your mind is possible*. I stare at it. It is advertising an afternoon seminar this weekend with a spiritual teacher. I grab a napkin from the counter and write down the number.

We drive out to the Dodgers Stadium to watch a baseball game. Albert is a touch on the quiet side. We pull into the car park and I have never seen so many cars and people in the one place in my life. Albert buys me a Dodgers cap to match his, and once we are in our seats I take a photo of the two of us with my phone.

'Oh, you don't want a picture of me,' Albert says.

'Yes, I do. It's going be my wallpaper.'

Albert gets us each a bucket of unshelled peanuts from the passing hawker. Everyone around us is also eating peanuts and throwing their shells on the ground. There is quite a large man next to me whose shells haven't made it past his stomach — and he has them all over his chest. I collect mine in my napkin, but Albert insists I have to throw them on the ground. I do, but feel guilty every time.

The game starts and the air is electric. The crowd is one huge blue blur. If a bowerbird flew into the stadium, it would go around in a circle, short circuit and drop dead. People hold up banners and scream as if their lives depend on this one game. Albert tries explaining the rules to me, but my eyes glaze over so I just cheer when he cheers. I watch the crowd more than the players. The screaming becomes deafening to the point where all I can hear is silence. I watch Albert as he gets up out of his chair, and throws his arms in the air. My eyes don't listen to me this time, and they fill with tears.

The following afternoon while I'm getting my make-up done, George stands at the sink behind me brushing his teeth.

'Have you ever brushed your teeth with earplugs in?' I say.

George shakes his head.

'You should try it.'

'Why?' he mumbles.

'Because it sounds like you are going through a car wash.'

He raises an eyebrow at me.

'You have to try it. It sounds so much like going through a car wash you won't believe it.'

He spits into the sink. 'I don't have any earplugs.'

'Here, I'll block your ears while you brush.'

I do.

'Wow, yeah, really, really amazing, Sunny.'

'It is! Do you want me to block your ears so you can try?' I ask the make-up artist as I sit back down.

She shakes her head. The top she wears clearly shows that she actually does have fake breasts. Teenage-looking face, teenage-looking breasts, and a forty-year-old neck.

Why go to all that trouble if you are going to skip the neck?

'Hey, don't you dare try and slip in the tongue tonight, Sunny,' George says.

This evening we are shooting the scene where Zoë and Ryan go for a late-night swim.

'Don't worry, I definitely won't.'

'I really need to feel safe with the person I'm working with in order to let my creativity flow. I need to be able to trust you and feel vulnerable with you, without worrying you might take advantage of me.'

I laugh, and the make-up artist looks back and forth between George and me, expressionlessly.

'I know Sunny seems all innocent,' George says to the make-up artist, 'but she's not. We were in a kissing scene together once and she went in for the dry root.'

'Oh, shut up, George, I did not. Don't listen to him.'

The make-up artist gives me an odd smile and clamps down on a bit of my eyelid with her eyelash curler. I pull away, which yanks my eyelashes and makes my eyes water. She recommends I get myself some permanent eyelash extensions and says they would really make my eyes 'pop' on screen.

'Action!' calls Katrina, our new director.

We run into the water; it's insanely cold. The more I try to stop my chattering teeth, the worse they get. The script goes out the window, because I'm too cold to remember my lines.

We improvise our dialogue and I instigate an impromptu handstand competition. George makes a comment on my goosebumps and goes to cuddle me. I try to push him away, but he keeps me there. He looks at me, brushes my wet hair out of my eyes and moves in for the kiss. I start wondering if George is going to slip his tongue in, which makes me start laughing. This sets George off, too, so Katrina calls cut.

'I forgot how amazing you two are together,' Katrina says. 'You do my job for me — that was fantastic. Really sweet scene.'

We pick up the kiss, and I am frozen to the bone. I go through the motions and want to get it over with as soon as possible. We finally wrap. I sit and defrost in the wardrobe van in front of the heater. Then Katrina takes George and me out for a beer.

'So what are you doing out here?' I ask her.

'I came over to meet with some rich people that are interested in investing in my film.'

'Is that the feature you wrote?' George asks.

'Yeah. No one in Australia wants to touch it. There's a part for both of you in it, as long as you aren't fifty by the time we make the bloody thing!' She has a wonderful loud cackle and always laughs at her own jokes in an insecure way. 'So how much longer are you guys planning to be here?'

'At least till my visa runs out, so another few years,' George says.

'And I'm going home next week,' I say.

'You didn't tell me that,' George says. 'When are you coming back?'

'I'm not sure, maybe never.'

'You can't do a couple of months here and then just leave. You have to stick it out. Go home and get your visa sorted, then come back and give it a good few years,' George says.

'I don't think I will. I don't think I'm America's cup of tea.'

'You are too good not to give it a proper go. If you'd done the equivalent body of work here as you have done in Australia, there would be a star map to your house. And it would be a huge fuck-off house. You don't want to be renting a shitbox flat for the rest of your life.'

'He's got a point there, Sunny. Why not chase the dollars here for a few years?' Katrina says.

'I think all of the things that got me work in Australia get steamrolled by the American accent. I feel like a big fat phony every time I do it,' I say.

'The accent becomes second nature in no time. You'd be crazy not to come back. It's a no-brainer; I'm not letting you give up on this place,' George says.

'I'm not happy here.'

'No one is,' George replies.

They continue to try to convince me, and I continue to make excuses. It gets late, we say our goodbyes and George walks me to my car. After I hop in, I wind down my window and ask him which is the best way to get home. I definitely came the long way round to get here; avoiding freeways has proven to be very time-consuming.

He gives me directions back to his house, not mine.

'Just come for one more drink,' he says.

'I can't. We have to be up early tomorrow.'

'Isn't it dangerous having to check for your freckle hand at night when you're following directions?'

'Yep.'

'Why don't you just make yourself learn? You're a smart girl.'

'Don't you think I've tried? It doesn't work; I can't learn.'

'Come on, just come back to mine for one tiny drink. You can follow me.'

'I really can't. I have to go home and have a hot bath and go to bed.'

'There's a bath and a bed at my house.'

I take a loud audible breath. 'You only want to sleep with me because you think it will be interesting for the film. It won't be, George. The lead-up is the interesting part. Once you actually have sex, the chemistry disappears, and what you're left with is awkwardness. If you want what's best for the film, you should just keep things the way they are now.'

'Who do you think I am, Sunny? This has nothing to do with the fucking film.'

'Don't lie. You couldn't care less about me before this film came along. I tried to contact you quite a few times, and you never called me back.'

'You want to know why I didn't call you? Because I like you,' he says in a primal-sounding voice that gives me a little shiver. 'Finally I see you and you're single and you made it very fucking clear you didn't want a bar of me.'

'What? Because I wouldn't sleep with you that night I spewed? I don't have one-night stands!' I have now matched the volume of George's raised voice. 'I know how this works; you are making up a story around me to fit in with the film. Then the next job will come along and you will move on to the next girl.'

'You really think I'm that fucked up? I couldn't give a shit about the film,' George says.

'You're married to your work. I know what goes

through your head, because it's the same thing that goes through mine. The script just happens to say that this character is the girl of your dreams, so in real life you look at me, and you try and work out how I could be that girl.'

'But I wrote this script, and I cast you,' he says, then turns and walks away.

Good line, George. Good exit.

I drive off into the darkness, and even the heater on its highest setting doesn't warm me up.

It is our last shoot day. We have to do the scene where
Ryan and Zoë go back to her place after their late-
night swim and have a bit of a romp. I step into make-up
and see George at the sink brushing his teeth. I smile at
him; he doesn't stop brushing but gives me a half-smile
back. I start brushing my teeth and we stare at each other,
brushing loudly. I am not going to apologise for last
night, and I am not going to be the first to look away. The
make-up artist opens the door, gives us an artificial grin
and busies herself in the corner.

'I was going to make up some new blue amendments
for today's scene that said "Zoë gives Ryan a blow job",
and get one of the PAs to hand them to you, but I didn't
think it would go down too well this morning,' George
says.

I can't think of anything clever to say so I laugh. The
make-up artist clears her throat.

'Action,' Katrina calls.

It is a closed set and the windows are blacked out to
make it look dark. There is no dialogue, and the agreement
is that we will basically be taking off each other's clothes
(down to underwear) and doing some kissing.

When I am driving fast down hills, I always wonder what it would feel like to accelerate and crash into the car in front of me. This is like a safe way to find out.

We burst into the room and tear each other's clothes off. George is a hard kisser and kisses with authority. He kisses me like his life depends on it and his gripping hands somehow dissolve my insecurities. I am suspended in time and there is no dripping tap.

George pulls away from the kiss and holds my face. He looks at me with such a fierce intensity, I almost have to look away. My god he is beautiful. Time stops and the silence throbs. We have been given a legal, guilt-free gift of each other with no consequences, like the way food becomes calorie-less if you eat it at the fridge with the fridge door open. It's as if I've been living in a straitjacket with my mouth taped shut, and now all of a sudden I am released.

I finally feel my mind kicking in and something telling me to pull back; it is the same voice that orders you to put your packet of cigarettes under the tap when you are trying to give up. Then another voice overrides it with: 'Why waste good cigarettes? They aren't free.' That second voice tells me not to pull out of this.

'Cut!'

Where did that come from? Who was that?

We stop and the wardrobe girl runs in to cover us both up.

'Wow,' Katrina says, fanning her face with her call sheet. 'Great scene, I definitely got what I need there.'

Is she sure? Only one take?

'It's only going to end up being quite a quick grab,' she adds.

In a dressing-gown, with burning cheeks, I stumble out into the day. I feel like I'm bursting, like I've just jumped out of a plane. I have no idea how to go back to walking at the mundane pace of life after that.

I go to my trailer and sit on the lounge, wondering what I need. Cigarettes? Sugar? Vodka? A shower? I light a cigarette, and blow the smoke out the back window, while staring straight at the *No Smoking* sign. I can't sit on the step outside, because I don't want to see George. I can't stop smiling. What was that? My god, I can still feel my heart beating.

I light a second cigarette and take long drags without breaths in between. Careful, I warn myself, lust is not love, chemistry is not love, and this isn't actually about George at all.

I creep over to craft service and stock up on an Eskimo Pie and some chocolate, and scamper back into my trailer. As I start on the Eskimo Pie, I hear a knock at the door. Shit. I really can't see George. I get up, tiptoe to the sink and stand up against the wall with my eyes half closed.

Another louder knock. Uh-oh. Persistent. I can't answer now, because I didn't answer it the first time.

'I can see you,' George yells.

Ah! I open my eyes, look out the window through the gap in the curtain and straight at George. Eek. Oh no, I am such an idiot. I open the door, with ice cream in hand.

'Are you hiding?' he asks.

'No.' I am a terrible, terrible actress and proper weirdo. 'I thought you were one of the ADs and I wasn't quite ready to come and do the next scene. So, yeah, I was hiding.'

'Right. We have about an hour before the next scene.'

'Oh, I didn't know that.'

More fabulous acting.

'Just wanted to apologise for last night.'

'Okay.'

'Okay,' he says, and walks away.

Oh dear. I stuff down the rest of the ice cream a bit too quickly. Better make a start on my chocolate bars; wouldn't want them to go to waste.

Luckily the last few scenes of the day are small. I am okay when I am actually acting, but in between takes I find it hard to talk to George.

We finally wrap and there is a big round of applause and everyone gives each other a hug.

My hug with George is very brief, and I am the first to move off.

'Are you coming for wrap drinks?' George asks, as he catches up to me.

'Depends. Is Dirk going to be there?'

'I didn't invite him. Why?'

'I was hoping to crack on.'

'You serious?' George asks.

'No, god, no.'

Again, awkward.

I walk into the bar, set up around a swimming pool. I pass a DJ and rows of sun beds, and find our little party in an open hut with a thatched roof. For something different, the place is filled with supermodels, who make me feel like a dumpy, middle-aged women, even in my favourite white dress.

In the same way Nurofen seeks out pain and targets it, my clever vodka seems to be following suit. All the crunchy parts of my mind start to vanish.

Katrina tells story after story, and her cackle gets louder with every drink. I decide I need some food, so I give the deep-fried mixed plate on our table a go. I get a thick greasy coating all over my mouth and I decide to smoke instead.

'Do you want to come for a quick trip to the toilet?' George asks.

'No.'

'Come on.' He stands, and I stand with him.

We walk into the men's toilets, and no one looks twice at me. We go into a cubicle and George takes out a bag of cocaine.

'Remember that night you had me over and I helped you with that scene where we had to pretend to snort cocaine in a toilet cubicle?' George asks in a whisper. I smile. 'Then you kissed me?'

'That was in the script,' I whisper back.

'I know, but we were practising a scene and you still chose to kiss me.'

We look at each other, then George starts to pour the white powder onto the toilet seat.

'Oh, shit. I nearly forgot. God. I can't have any, none for me,' I say, still whispering. 'The last time I had cocaine in this country, I ended up in hospital.'

'What? When? You didn't tell me that.'

'It's a long story.'

'This is the best you can get. I promise you will be fine with this stuff.'

'No, really, I can't,' I say.

George has his line, then mine, and suggests we go and sit up at the bar for Fernet-Branca shots.

'Booked your flight back here yet?' George asks.

'No. I don't think I am coming back.'

'You have to. Come back and live with me.'

'We'd kill each other.'

'We wouldn't, you know.'

'Yes, we would.'

'Have you ever thought about us?' George asks, staring intently at one of the calluses on his hand.

'Yeah,' I say.

'And?'

'Yes, we're screamingly perfect together when we are under the right lights with a moving soundtrack, but does that translate into real life?'

'I dunno.'

'Once reality kicked in and you saw my cellulite and how psychotic I get when I'm premenstrual, you'd run a mile.'

'Why is it that you love to sit and tell me how I really feel, or how I will feel in the future?'

'Because I know how you think.'

'Well, how about I tell you what I really think? Ready? I think we should give it a go,' George says.

'What are you actually proposing? You want to sleep with me? Because you have offered that a few times now and I have declined every time.'

George looks away from me.

'There are a lot of pretty girls here. I'm sure any one of them would go home with you.'

Oops, I think I did step over the mark with that last bit.

'You are unbelievable,' George says, putting his head in his hands. 'I'm trying to tell you I like you and you bite my fucking head off.' George orders another drink, then we go back to join the others.

I don't want to be here anymore. To my surprise there are no protests as I get up and say my goodbyes.

As the valet brings my car around, I am thanking god I didn't continue to drink myself over the limit. I drive off and can't stop thinking about the feeling I had today, after the scene where I kissed George.

Is that sort of feeling what stopped me from saying yes to marrying Tobey?

The funny thing is, that feeling I had isn't actually real. It's about me wanting what I don't have, and that temptation is a mirage created by my mind to keep me from being happy with my current situation. It's like a rainbow — it can't be bottled and taken home.

I get home and go down to the house to find something to eat. I creep in and see Albert sitting in an armchair in the dark, looking out the side window. He has a scotch in his hand.

'Albert? Are you okay?'

'Yes, my dear, having a little night cap.'

'What are you thinking about?' I ask as I kneel down on the floor next to his chair.

'Pearl,' he says quietly with a smile.

'I'm sure she is somewhere lovely, with lots of tea.'

He smiles again. 'Sometimes I'm not sure why I am still hanging around here,' he says, and I get a slightly winded feeling in my throat.

'There are so many reasons why you're here, Albert. Look at what you've done for me. You've saved me.'

'No, you've saved me.'

Left side, no. Right side, no. Stomach, no. Doona off, no. If only I had a recording of Tobey's snore; it's the one thing that guarantees sleep. I try a special yoga position, drink too much chamomile tea, go on my computer, read my book and finally get some sleep in the early hours of the morning, with the lamp on.

I wake up with a numb headache and call Nina, to see if she wants to go and drink too much coffee with me. She declines, saying she has too much to do. I decide to put together my own list of things that need to be done before I get on the plane in less than a week's time. I start on my washing mound. As I go to put my jeans in the machine, I find that napkin with the phone number for the spiritual-teacher seminar in a pocket. Maybe this could be the little slice of India I missed out on by coming to America instead? Seeing as I have nothing planned for Sunday afternoon, I decide to call the number and book in.

I expect a little room in a rundown hall somewhere but come across quite the opposite. I enter a spiritual paradise with colourful Buddhist flags flying out the front, an organic café, books and music in the 'marketplace', and even a 'wellness centre' where you can 'pop in' for a facial, massage or acupuncture treatment.

I register at the front desk, and the woman asks for my name three times. Maybe she can't hear me over the loud music (some sort of chanting) or maybe she can't understand my accent. Either way she looks extremely annoyed, which goes against the bindi on her forehead and the mandala beads around her neck.

I have some time to fill, so I get myself some lunch from the café. I order a drink called 'kombucha', and a tempeh and lentil stew-type scenario. The drink has to be the foulest thing I have ever tasted; the label says it's a tea that has been fermented using a solid mass of microorganisms, called a 'kombucha colony', and aids digestion and healing. It tastes like a fizzy version of bile. I make myself have a couple more sips, then throw it in the bin. I force down my stew, which is only a slight step up from my drink, but leave the large chunks of undercooked eggplant. I go for a wander and look at all the spiritual paraphernalia in the marketplace.

I enter the room where the workshop is taking place. It is silent and full of people sitting and meditating. Uh-oh. Prime giggle territory. I grab a cushion and find a spot near the front next to a young blonde-haired woman who puts her hands together and bows her head at me.

Am I supposed to do that back? For some reason I don't feel like I have the right, seeing as I'm neither Indian nor Japanese. I smile and turn away, hoping she doesn't think I'm rude. I sit with my eyes closed for what seems like days. I keep peeking to see if anything new has happened. I check my phone, just to make sure it's still on silent, and to see if anyone has called in the last ten minutes. I look around the room. Some people are in robe-type clothing, some have white turbans on their heads, and others are in jeans.

Finally I open my eyes and the spiritual teacher from the photograph has appeared on the stage, with her eyes closed. She is exquisitely beautiful and sits on a white couch next to a bunch of orange flowers. She wears white with bright blue turquoise beads around her neck, and I can't stop staring at her. Is it the anticipation that makes her seem so special? Is it the set-up? I get this same sort of feeling when I'm at a church or a concert.

At last she opens her eyes, taps some cymbals together, clasps her hands in prayer and looks around the room. Everyone else also has his or her hands in prayer, so this time I follow suit. Feels quite good actually. Everyone is either smiling or crying, and it seems as if the room is vibrating.

'I have an invitation for everyone here.'

For some reason I didn't expect her to have an American accent.

'An invitation to switch your allegiance from the activities of your mind to the presence of your being. It can happen in this moment,' she says.

Is that possible? Is there a choice not to be at your mind's mercy? I am so used to my mind eating me alive.

She goes on to talk about her guru, who had a head twitch. When asked about it, he said: 'When an elephant gets into a tent, something's got to give.'

I think of Sam. I wonder if he always had his twitch or if it just developed after the drinking and the fame.

She says that she has spent her life chasing an idea of 'enlightenment' or 'fulfilment', but has now realised in her furious searching that peace and freedom have been there all along and are not things that can be 'discovered' outside of yourself.

Does that apply to me, too? Or just her?

The afternoon drifts on, and my concentration goes in and out, but there is one sentence that sticks in my mind: 'All you need to do in this lifetime is find out what truly makes you happy and follow it.'

That night I make thin-crust potato and rosemary pizza from scratch (a secret recipe from an old Italian flatmate). Albert is beside himself and says it is the best thing he has ever eaten, then looks up at the sky and apologises to Pearl.

'What did you learn at your seminar?' he asks.

'Um, I think I sell myself out. Whenever I meet someone new I try and mould myself into who I think they want me to be.'

'Why do you think that is?'

'Partly because I want everyone to like me, but also because I don't think I really know who I am. Sometimes I think I don't even know what my taste is. I looked through the music on my iPod, the other day and saw stuff on there that I don't even like. None of the songs that really secretly move me are on there.'

'Give me an example of one that really moves you.'

'"You're the Voice" by John Farnham.'

'Can't say I've ever heard of him.'

'He's Australian. Growing up, whenever I got to make

a wish on an eyelash, I'd always wish that one day I'd end up marrying him. That is actually quite creepy because he's twice my age.'

'What do you wish for now?'

'I don't know, Albert. Lately I have just been wishing for silence. Things have been pretty noisy for a while.'

The following morning I wake up and head to Fred Segal to spend the voucher Albert gave me for my birthday on a dress for the wedding. Thank god we'll get to be barefoot so I don't have to worry about shoes. I get an armload of dresses to try on and narrow it down to a red dress (which is a bit short and kind of slutty) and a silk royal-blue one. I change from one to the other, unable to decide which direction I want to go in.

I get a text from George saying he has money for me and wondering when he should drop it off. I text him back and tell him where I am, and he suggests we meet at a nearby café in an hour.

The overexcited sales assistant insists I go with the red one, telling me how 'cute' it is on me. That one word alone makes me decide on the blue one.

Waiting for George, I rapidly tap my foot on my chair leg and sip on my iced coffee, cursing myself for forgetting to ask for no whipped cream. I pretend to be engrossed in my boring magazine but check the door of the café every few seconds to see if George has walked in.

Finally he strolls in. He gives me a quick kiss on the cheek, and hands me an envelope of cash.

'Worth every cent,' he says in a dirty-old-man voice.

I laugh, then apologise for being mean to him at the wrap drinks, and he says it's okay and that he's used to it.

He goes to the counter to order and comes back with a cupcake with blue icing. He offers me a bite, which I decline because I can't eat anything blue.

He tells me how happy he is with my performance and the film's rushes. We wade through surface conversation and George spends most of the time looking down at his hands.

'Do you think that's true?' George asks as he walks me to my car, pointing to my faded old T-shirt that reads *All you need is love* across the front.

'Yeah,' I say and smile. 'Do you?'

'Yep,' he says quickly and gives me a hug goodbye.

'If you do decide to come back, I'm here. Okay?'

'Okay.' I drive off into the afternoon.

When something you think you wanted finally gets handed to you, it's amazing the way the glitter falls off. I turn the music up and go through more orange lights than I usually would.

The drive to the airport is too quiet; it's as if I'm leading them both to their death. Albert drives with his eyes fixed on the road. I am in the front seat and Nina is in the back staring out the window with luggage all over her. I made Albert promise he wouldn't park and come in with us, partly because of the paying-for-parking thing, and partly because I cannot bear long goodbyes.

We pull up outside the airport. As Albert opens the

car boot, his shirtsleeve slips up and I see a sweatband on his wrist.

'Oh, Albert!' I say and my bottom lip starts quivering.

He gives me a hug. 'I'm going to miss you kiddo,' he says into my hair.

'I'm going to miss you more. You have no idea what you've done for me. I have so much to thank you for.'

Words seem like big clumsy clichés that go nowhere near explaining the depth of gratitude and love that I have for this man. I imagine Albert driving home to an empty house, and get an enormous wave of guilt. I have to turn and walk away a couple of steps. Albert follows me and hugs me again.

'I'm so sorry I'm leaving you. I always seem to be leaving,' I say in a high-pitched voice, with tears dripping down my face.

'Oh, don't worry about me. I'll be fine,' he says, still hugging me.

'Hey, we better go,' Nina says gently.

She's right, we are running late. I fish around in my bag and find Albert's little present.

'It's only tiny, I didn't know what to get you.' I pass him a wrapped framed photo of the two of us. In turn he passes me an envelope, which I put straight into my bag. 'If you ever come to Australia, look me up!' I yell out, as we walk away. I keep turning back and waving until he is out of sight.

Our Qantas flight is relatively empty, so Nina and I move up the back and find a free row of seats to ourselves. We have plastic glasses of New Zealand sauvignon blanc in our hands, and I cannot stop smiling at the sound of the Australian accent all around me.

Our dinner arrives and Nina looks longingly at my meatballs and mash.

'I told you not to order vegan; all you ever get is rice cakes.' I share my meal with her, even down to giving her half of my little Cadbury bar. 'I think it's the right move coming home,' I say.

'Yeah, I guess. Sometimes it's so hard to just trust my gut.'

'I know what you mean. I find it so difficult to decipher between my instincts and that naughty part of my mind that wears a name tag saying "instinct" on it.'

'If I trusted the one with the name tag, I would be at a pancake-eating competition every second day.'

We go into our own little worlds and watch movie after movie. Nina takes a sleeping tablet and drops straight to sleep. I say no to a tablet and therefore cannot sleep. I remember Albert's envelope and find it in my bag. Inside there is a pair of earplugs and a note that reads: *This is me granting your wish, put these in for instant silence, x Albert.*

I pop them in and finally fall into an odd half-sleep.

I wake up with a stiff neck and a blocked nose. I squeeze past Nina, who is dead to the world, and make my way to the toilets. It's so eerie to be up in the sky in such a small space with so many sleeping people everywhere. I wash my face and do some stretches in the aisle. I strap myself back into my hard narrow seat, which is worlds away from business class, and stare out the window into the blackness.

I don't actually need to be in business class, just like

I don't actually need to be famous. I think I have been driven by an old set of childhood desires that don't bear much resemblance to the person I am today. In the same way you sometimes go through a long stage of forgetting to buy a new toothbrush, I have gone through a long stage without upgrading the list of what I really want.

Finally we step onto Australian soil. I see something in Nina's smile that I haven't seen for a while. Her mum is there to meet us, and I watch her fingertips whiten as she grips onto Nina in a very tight hug. Then she grabs me and thanks me for bringing her daughter home.

The plane to Ballina is tiny and registers every bump and wind pocket, which gives me sweaty palms for the entire flight. I take an extra-large handful of the mixed lollies that are passed around in a small cane basket and eat them in quick succession. Mum tried to insist on meeting me at the airport, but seeing as I wouldn't fit in much time with her before the wedding, I told her it was best to come tomorrow.

I sit in the front seat of a taxi from Ballina Airport to Byron Bay. The weather is perfect, and the way the air changes when you drive into this town is like magic. My god I love this country.

I ask the taxi driver where the best coffee is, and he stops there so that I can get a takeaway soy latte. Finally! A coffee that tastes like liquid gold, as opposed to liquid dirt. We arrive at my little bed and breakfast on Wategos

Beach, right across the road from the water. Wow — it is as gorgeous as it looked on the website. In the lounge room there are terracotta tiles and big white Balinese daybeds. There are glass French doors that open out onto the deck, which looks out over palm trees and the ocean. I am in paradise. This place is way too expensive, but I thought for one night it could be my little treat.

In the bedroom there is a wooden four-poster bed with a mosquito net. I have a flop on the bed and eat the chocolates that are nestled into the pillow, lying down with my eyes closed. I feel as if I could sleep for days. I don't let myself and instead put my cossies on and dive into the ocean. The water is warm and makes me feel like I have had a full blood transfusion.

I drag myself out of the water and back to my room. I check the time and realise I only have half an hour to get ready. Shit.

I have a quick shower, put on my new blue dress and apply my beauty flash balm, which is only for special occasions. As I put on mascara I notice my hand is shaking.

I pop my thongs in my bag and walk barefoot with wet hair along Wategos Beach, up over the hill, and down towards Little Wategos. I see the wedding congregation in the distance and hear a guitar playing. I focus on the hot grey sea of rocks that I need to cross before I get onto the sand.

I have prickles all over my skin, my hands are still shaking, and the jet lag is starting to hit. I carefully tread from one rock to the next, not able to look up in case I trip or see Tobey.

I step off the last rock, look up and straight at him.

He is in a suit standing next to the groom, facing the wedding party. He looks right back at me, as I am walking in the direction of the aisle towards him. For a moment my heart forgets what its rhythm is and for a moment I could almost be walking up to marry him.

My life has never really looked like a fairy tale, and maybe I have to pay the price for taking the time to make my decision. Maybe he has a date with him or maybe he might just grab me and take me home. I have no idea what's about to happen but at least now I know what I want.

Acknowledgements

Thank you Aviva Tuffield for taking a risk w
seamlessly rearranging my endless add-ins, and
patience with my terrible spelling. Without you th
would still be on grubby scraps of paper in my
drawer.

Also thank you to Scribe Publications, Peter B
my beautiful family, Damon Gameau, Emma M
Jennifer Naughton, Tracey Silvester and everyone e
RGM.

Lastly, this book would never have been written
wasn't for Conor Reid: thank you for making me la
nonstop and telling me I can do anything.